MW00912623

WORKBOOK 2

Louis Fidge

MACMILLAN

Contents

Words about my body

Read the meaning of
each word.

Then fill in the missing
vowels in the words.

There are **five vowels.**
They are:

a e i o u

Every word must contain **at
least one** vowel.

a) h e a r t   This pumps blood around our bodies.

b) l _ n g s   These help us to breathe.

c) b r a i n   This helps us to think.

d) s k _ l _ t _ n   This is made of bones.

e) c h _ s t   Our heart is inside this.

f) s k _ l l   Our brain is inside this.

g) b _ n _ s   There are over 200 of these in our
body.

h) b l _ _ d   Our heart pumps this round our body.

i) b r _ _ t h _   Our lungs help us to do this.

j) t h _ n k   Our brain helps us to do this.

4

Putting the words in order

These words are in **alphabetical order**, according to their **first letters**:

      brother   **f**ather   **m**other

These words are in **alphabetical order**, according to their **second letters**:

      b**a**th   b**e**d   b**r**other

1 Write these words in alphabetical order, according to their first letters.

a) skeleton   heart   brain

brain   _heart_   _skeleton_

b) lungs   blood   chest

blood   _chest_   _lungs_

c) think   pump   breathe

breathe   _pump_   _think_

d) girl   boy   child

boy   _child_   _girl_

2 Write these words in alphabetical order, according to their second letters.

a) chest   carrot   clock

carrot   _chest_   _clock_

b) skin   short   send

send   _short_   _skin_

c) beat   breathe   bird

beat   _bird_   _breathe_

d) diet   drink   danger

danger   _diet_   _drink_

Some common words

Remember

Some words are very **common**.
We use them a lot.
Can you see **hen** in 'w**hen**'?

them	they	there	that	then
these	here	where	what	when

a) Write all the words that begin with **the**.

Them, they, There, other

b) Write all the words with **hat** in them.

That, What

c) Write all the words with **here** in them.

There, where

d) Write all the words with **hen** in them.

Then, when

e) Write all the words with **he** in them.

Then, when, There, them

f) Write all the words that begin with **th**.

They, then

g) Write all the words that begin with **wh**.

when

Cover each word up one at a time and try to write it
from memory, without copying.

Then, what, here, them

My body

Copy the sentences.
Begin each sentence
with a capital letter.

End each sentence
with a full stop.

A sentence **begins** with a
capital letter. Many sentences
end with a **full stop**.
A skeleton is made of bones.

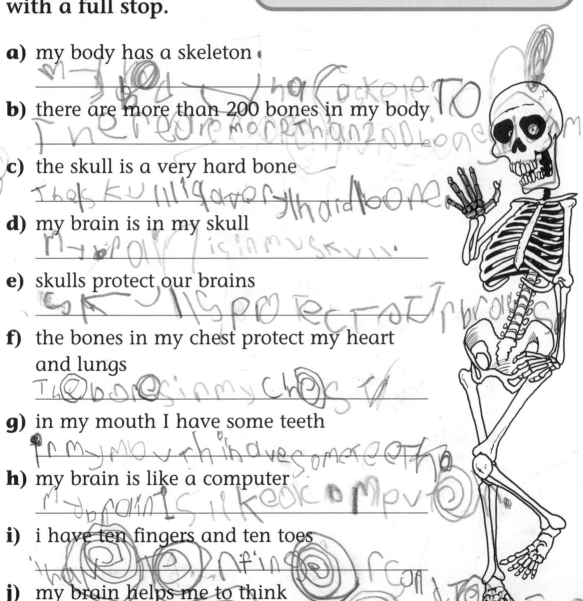

a) my body has a skeleton

b) there are more than 200 bones in my body

c) the skull is a very hard bone

d) my brain is in my skull

e) skulls protect our brains

f) the bones in my chest protect my heart
and lungs

g) in my mouth I have some teeth

h) my brain is like a computer

i) i have ten fingers and ten toes

j) my brain helps me to think

Feelings

Remember

The sentences below are all about feelings.

Write the words in these sentences in the right order.

Sentences must **make sense**.

girl the sad is. ✗

The girl is sad. ✓

Begin each sentence with a capital letter.

End each sentence with a full stop.

a) happy feel I

I feel Happy

b) boy the excited looks

The boy looks excited

c) my angry mum is

my mum is angry

d) felt my tired grandfather

my grandad felt tired

e) was film the boring

The film was boring

f) the pleased was girl with her story

The girl was pleased with her story

g) night at sometimes afraid feel I

I feel afraid at night sometimes

h) sad was I my when died pet

I was sad when my pet died

I and me

When I talk about **myself**, I use the words **I** and **me**.

I have a brain. It helps **me** to think.

1 Write the correct word in each gap.

a) ___I___ (I, me) have a brain. It helps ___me___ (I, me) to think.

b) May ___I___ (I, me) have a cake, please?

c) Mum gave ___me___ (I, me) a present.

d) Throw the ball to ___me___ (I, me). _____ (I, me) will catch it.

e) Look at ___me___ (I, me). ___I___ (I, me) am very wet.

f) ___I___ (I, Me) have two lungs. They help ___me___ (I, me) breathe.

2 Write each sentence correctly.

a) Me would like a drink.

I would like a drink

b) Will you give I a sweet if me ask nicely?

Will you give me a sweet nicely?

c) Me ran very fast.

I ran very fast.

d) Me like it when you call for I to play.

I like it when you call me to play.

e) Me got good marks at school. The teacher was pleased with I.

I got good marks at school the teacher was pleased

f) My brother and me are playing in the yard.

My brother and me playing in the yard

My and mine

Remember

When something **belongs to me**, I use the words **my** or **mine**.

This is **my** cricket bat. It is **mine**.

1 **Write the correct word in each gap.**

   a) I have lots of teeth in _my_ (my, mine) mouth.

   b) _My_ (My, Mine) heart sends blood round _my_ (my, mine) body.

   c) The red bag is _mine_ (my, mine).

   d) Don't eat that cake! It is _mine_ (my, mine).

   e) _My_ (My, Mine) skeleton is made of bones.

   f) The yellow cap belongs to Carl, but the white cap is _mine_ (me, mine).

2 **Write each sentence correctly.**

   a) The book belongs to me. It is my.

   The book belongs to me. It is mine.

   b) Tom loves his school. I love my, too.

   Tom loves his school I love mine

   c) I can read mine book easily.

   I can read my book easily.

   d) Jim's birthday is in March. Mine birthday is in May.

   Jim's birthday is in March my birthday is in May.

   e) Mine teacher is very nice.

   My teacher is very nice

You read a book

Doing words are called **verbs**.
A **verb** tells us what someone or
something is **doing**.
You **read** a book.

1 **Write the correct verb in
each sentence.**

comb	read	bang
sing	tie	eat

a) You _read_ a book.

b) You _sing_ a song.

c) You _tie_ a knot.

d) You _comb_ your hair

e) You _bang_ a drum.

f) You _eat_ a sandwich.

2 **Think of a suitable verb to fill in each gap.**

a) You p_aint_ a picture.

b) You c_limb_ a ladder.

c) You r_ide_ a bike.

d) You m_owed_ the grass.

e) You c_atch_ a ball.

f) You s_leep_ in a bed.

11

Some noisy animals!

Remember

A **verb** is a **doing word**.
Sometimes a verb ends with '**s**'.

A hummingbird **hums**.

1 Underline the verb in each sentence.

a) The man <u>knocks</u> on the door.

b) The girl <u>paints</u> a picture.

c) The lady <u>picks</u> up her bag.

d) The frog <u>hops</u> onto the rock.

e) The man <u>eats</u> his lunch.

f) He <u>jumps</u> over the wall.

2 Add 's' to the end of each verb. Complete each sentence with the correct form of the verb.

a) A goat _brays_ (bray).

b) A cow _moos_ (moo).

c) A lion _roars_ (roar).

d) A dog _barks_ (bark).

e) A duck _quacks_ (quack).

f) A frog _croaks_ (croak).

g) A parrot _squawks_ (squawk).

h) An elephant _trumpets_ (trumpet).

i) A monkey _chatters_ (chatter).

j) A mouse _squeaks_ (squeak).

Naming words

Naming words are called **nouns**.

chair

book

girl

The words **girl**, **chair** and **book** are **names** of things.
They are **nouns**.

frog	car	tap	hen	clock
plate	door	bird	bike	fish

Choose the correct noun to fill in each gap.

a) A c_lock_ tells us the time.

b) A f_ish_ swims in water.

c) A c_ar_ goes on a road.

d) A b_ike_ has got two wheels.

e) A f_rog_ can hop.

f) A b_ird_ can fly.

g) We put food on a p_late_.

h) We get eggs from a h_en_.

i) We get water from a t_ap_.

j) You go through a d_oor_.

More naming words

Remember

Naming words are called **nouns**.

ant

apple

The words **ant** and **apple** are **nouns**.

1 **Choose the correct noun for each gap.**
 a) You eat an _apple_. (apple, chair)
 b) You sit on a _chair_. (book, chair)
 c) You draw with a _pencil_. (car, pencil)
 d) You drive a _car_. (chair, car)
 e) You sleep in a _bed_. (pencil, bed)
 f) You read a _book_. (book, bed)

2 **Think of a suitable noun for each sentence.**
 a) I write with a _pencil_.
 b) I dig with a _spade_.
 c) I bang a _drum_.
 d) I climb a _tree_.
 e) I look out of a _window_.
 f) I throw a _ball_.
 g) I cut with a _knife_.
 h) I drink from a _mug_.

'a' or 'an'?

Remember

We use **an** in front of a noun that begins with a **vowel**.
There are **five vowels**: **a   e   i   o   u**

 an apple

We use **a** in front of a noun that begins with a **consonant**.
All letters that are **not vowels** are called **consonants**.

a bone

1 Write 'a' or 'an' in front of each noun.

a) _a_ ant   **b)** _an_ egg

c) _an_ ice-cream   **d)** _an_ orange

e) _an_ umbrella   **f)** _a_ tooth

g) _a_ bone   **h)** _a_ skeleton

i) _a_ star   **j)** _a_ brain

k) _an_ ape   **l)** _a_ heart

2 Choose 'a' or 'an' to fill each gap.

a) I saw _an_ ostrich in _a_ zoo.

b) _a_ boy has got _an_ apple.

c) _an_ ant is _an_ insect.

d) _a_ cat is _an_ animal.

e) There is _an_ egg on _a_ plate.

f) _a_ girl is eating _an_ orange.

15

A noun may be **singular** or **plural**.

one bone   lots of bones

Singular means **one** thing.   Plural means **more than one** thing.

We often **add 's'** to the **end** of a noun to make it **plural**.

1 **Add 's' to each singular noun to make it plural.**

a) one book – lots of ___books___

b) one shoe – lots of _shoes_

c) one cake – lots of _cakes_

d) one coat – lots of _coats_

e) one sweet – lots of _sweets_

f) one hat – lots of _hats_

g) one sock – lots of _socks_

h) one dog – lots of _dogs_

2 **Write the singular form of each noun.**

a) one ___cup___ – lots of cups

b) one _plate_ – lots of plates

c) one _spoon_ – lots of spoons

d) one _fork_ – lots of forks

e) one _chair_ – lots of chairs

f) one _table_ – lots of tables

g) one _bag_ – lots of bags

h) one _pencil_ – lots of pencils

One dish – lots of dishes

Remember

A noun may be **singular** (one thing) or **plural** (more than one thing).
When a noun ends in '**s**', '**x**', '**ch**' or '**sh**' we add '**es**' to make it plural.

one dish

lots of dishes

1 **Add 'es' to each noun to make it plural.**

a) brush   _brushes_   b) bench   _benches_

c) glass   _glasses_   d) box   _boxes_

e) bus   _buses_   f) fox   _foxes_

g) bush   _bushes_   h) church   _churches_

i) lunch   _lunches_   j) class   _classes_

k) six   _sixes_   l) crash   _crashes_

2 **Write some sentences of your own.**
Use five of the plural nouns you made above in your sentences.

I drive on the bus.

I can't to six.

I eat lunch.

I go to class.

A tall building

Remember

An **adjective** is a **describing** word. This adjective tells us more about the building.

a **tall** building

1 Choose the best adjective for each gap.

a) a _____ (yellow, blue) banana

b) a _____ (white, red) tomato

c) some _____ (black, green) grass

d) a _____ (sharp, wide) pencil

e) a _____ (soft, heavy) rock

f) a _____ (long, wet) snake

2 Draw the pictures. Underline the adjectives.

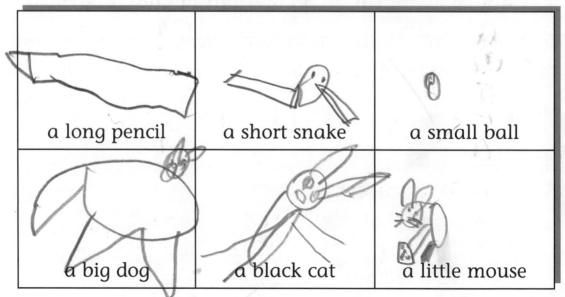

| a long pencil | a short snake | a small ball |
| a big dog | a black cat | a little mouse |

A big boy

Remember

An **adjective** is a **describing** word.

a **big** boy

an **unhappy** girl

1 Underline the adjectives.

a) I saw a <u>tall</u> ostrich with long legs.

b) Sam had a <u>cool</u> drink from a <u>glass</u> bottle.

c) There is a <u>big black</u> cloud in the sky.

d) The <u>small</u> child was playing with the new toys.

e) The <u>old</u> man read an interesting book.

f) The <u>noisy</u> children ran down the <u>busy</u> road.

2 Choose 'a' or 'an' to go in front of each adjective.

a) _a_ hot day

b) _a_ empty bottle

c) _an_ old man

d) _an_ interesting book

e) _a_ smooth stone

f) _a_ ugly toad

g) _an_ amazing adventure

h) _an_ open door

i) _a_ dark wood

j) _an_ angry man

3 Write these phrases correctly.

a) an large house _A large house._

b) a exciting film _An exciting film._

c) an tall building _A tall building._

19

Ordinal adjectives

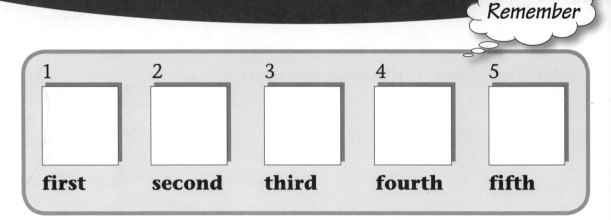

Remember

1	2	3	4	5
first	second	third	fourth	fifth

1 **Draw five cars in a line in the box below.**

- Colour the first car red.
- Colour the third car blue.
- Colour the fifth car green.
- Colour the second car yellow.
- Colour the fourth car orange.

red yellow blue orange green

2 **Answer these questions.**
   a) What colour is the first car? red
   b) What colour is the last car? orange
   c) What colour is the car in the middle? blue
   d) What colour is the car behind the first car? yellow
   e) What colour is the car in front of the last car?
   f) What colour is the car between the second and fourth cars?

green
orang
yellow

20

Can you walk on tip-toe?

Reading with understanding is an important **skill**.

1 Read this action rhyme.

Can you walk on tip-toe?

Can you walk on tip-toe,
As softly as a cat?
Can you stamp like an elephant,
Tramp, tramp, tramp, like that?

Can you hop, skip, jump,
Like a fat frog on the ground?
Can you slither through the grass,
Like a snake, without a sound?

Can you take great long strides,
Like a long-legged giraffe?
Can you be a hyena,
And laugh and laugh and laugh?

2 Now read it again and act it out as you do so.

3 The rhyme contains lots of verbs about animals moving.

Underline the verbs in the rhyme.

Small, smaller, smallest!

An **adjective** is a **describing** word.
Sometimes we use adjectives to **compare** things.

The snail is **small**.

The beetle is **smaller**.

The ant is **smallest**.

Anna   Sam   Mary   Ben

Look at the picture and answer these questions:

a) Is Ben taller than Mary? _yes_

b) Is Anna taller that Sam? _no_

c) Who is taller – Sam or Mary? _Mary_

d) Who is the tallest child? _Ben_

e) Is Anna shorter than Ben? _yes_

f) Is Mary shorter than Sam? _no_

g) Who is shorter – Mary or Anna? _Anna_

h) Who is the shortest child? _Anna_

Wild, wilder, wildest!

Remember

An **adjective** is a **describing** word.
Sometimes we use adjectives to **compare** things.

An elephant
is **wild**.

A tiger
is **wilder**.

A lion
is **wildest**.

1 Add 'er' to each adjective.

   a) high   _higher_   **b)** thick   *thicker*

   c) straight   *straighter*   **d)** clean   *cleaner*

   e) warm   *warmer*   **f)** quiet   *quieter*

   g) fast   *faster*   **h)** old   *older*

2 Complete this chart.

	adjective	add 'er'	add 'est'
a)	small	smaller	smallest
b)	wild	*wilder*	*wildest*
c)	soft	*softer*	*softest*
d)	round	*rounder*	*roundest*
e)	sharp	*sharper*	*sharpest*
f)	smooth	*smoother*	*smoothest*
g)	slow	*slower*	*slowest*
h)	hard	*harder*	*hardest*

I live in Jamaica

A **proper noun** is the name of a **particular person**, **place** or **thing**. A proper noun always **begins** with a **capital letter**.

My name is **Lenny**. I live in **Jamaica**.

Remember

1 Write the names of these people correctly. Begin each name with a capital letter.

ben　　　　**anna**　　　**mr brown**　　**mrs brown**

Ben　　Anna　　MrBrown mrsbrown

2 Copy the names of the days correctly. Write them in the correct order. Begin with Sunday.

Sunday

Monday
Tuesday
Wednesday
Thursday Thursday
Friday Friday
Saturday Saturdy

wednesday

tuesday

friday

saturday

sunday

thursday

monday

24

My name is ...

Remember

> A **proper noun** is the name of a **particular person**, **place** or **thing**.
> A proper noun always **begins** with a **capital letter**.

1 Copy these sentences. Put in the missing capital letters.

a) mr and mrs fisher went to jamaica.

Mr and mrs fisher went to Jamaica

b) mary lives in montego bay.

Mary lives in montego Bay

c) when i was ill doctor banks came to see me.

When I was ill doctor Banks came to see me

d) it is wednesday today.

It is Wednesday today

e) lizzy and lenny are twins.

Lizzy and Lenny are Twins twins

f) there are thirty one days in january.

There are thirty one days January

2 Fill in each gap with information about yourself.

My name is _____ Scout Mae _____.
My birthday is in the month of _____ June _____.
The name of my best friend is _____.
I go to _____ School.
The name of my teacher is _____.
The town I live in is called _____.
The country I live in is called _____.

Opposites

Remember

Opposites are words whose meanings are as **different** as possible from each other.

happy   sad

Match the pairs of opposites.   **Write them here.**

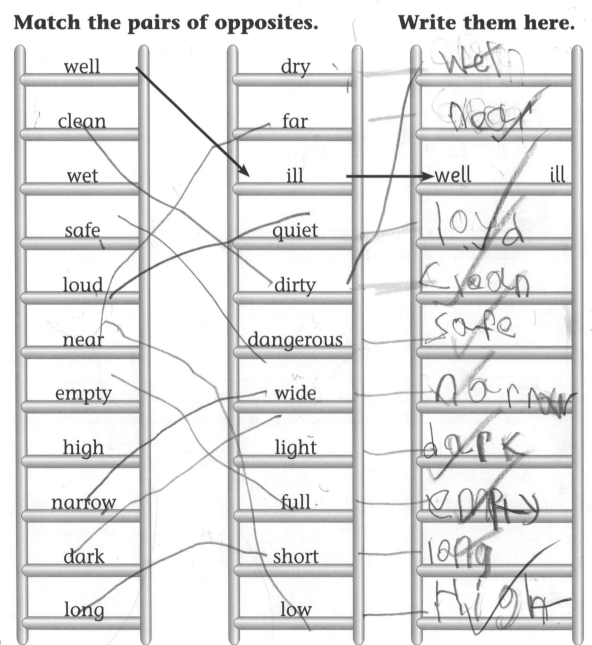

Match		Opposite	Written
well		dry	weт
clean		far	near
wet		ill	well ill
safe		quiet	loud
loud		dirty	clean
near		dangerous	safe
empty		wide	narrow
high		light	dark
narrow		full	early
dark		short	long
long		low	High

26

Open or shut?

Opposites are words whose meanings are as **different** as possible from each other, e.g. happy, sad.

1 **Choose the best adjective to complete each sentence.**

> shut   dry   cold
> near   slow   quiet

a) A hare can run fast but a tortoise is _slow_.

b) Fire is hot but ice is _cold_.

c) When it rains it is wet but when the sun comes out it is _dry_.

d) One door is open but one door is _shut_.

e) Some children are noisy but some children are _quiet_.

f) My uncle lives far away but my aunt lives _near_.

2 **Now try these.**

> sour   huge   long   dirty   soft   dark

a) An ant is small but a hippo is _huge_.

b) A rock is hard but cotton wool is _soft_.

c) My shirt is clean but my friend's shirt is _dirty_.

d) Sugar is sweet but a lemon is _sour_.

e) It is light in the day but it is _dark_ at night.

f) A centimetre is a short distance but a kilometre is a _long_ way.

Health and safety words

Remember

Read the meaning of each word.

Then fill in the missing vowels in the words.

> There are **five vowels**.
> They are:
>
> **a e i o u**
>
> Every word must contain **at least one** vowel.

a) h _e_ _a_ l t h — how someone feels – either well or ill

b) s _a_ f _e_ — the opposite of dangerous

c) d _i_ _e_ t — the food we eat

d) m _e_ d _i_ c _i_ n _e_ — we take this to make us better

e) _i_ l l — the opposite of well

f) c l _e_ _a_ n — the opposite of dirty

g) d _a_ n g _e_ r _ou_ s — not safe

h) d _o_ c t _o_ r — someone we go to see if we are not well

i) n _u_ r s _e_ — someone who looks after us when we are ill

j) _A_ c c _i_ d _e_ n t — something bad that happens that is not meant to happen

Remember

Naming words are
called **nouns**.
The words **doctor**
and **hospital**
are **names** of things.
They are **nouns**.

A **doctor** works
in a **hospital**.

1 Choose the
correct noun
for each gap.

hospital	medicine	
ambulance	stethoscope	nurse
heart	doctor	bed

a) A d <u>octor</u> works in a h <u>ospital</u>. ✓

b) A n <u>urse</u> takes care of us. ✓

c) When we are ill, we stay in b <u>ed</u> ✓.

d) Sometimes when we are ill, we take m <u>edicine</u> to
make us better. ✓

e) You can listen to your h <u>eart</u> with a s <u>tethoscope</u> ✓

f) An a <u>mbulance</u> takes you to the hospital. ✓

2 Choose the best noun to complete each sentence.

a) My house has got a <u>roof</u> ✓ (roof, loaf).

b) I sat down on the <u>chair</u> ✓ (pen, chair).

c) The <u>sun</u> (tree, sun) was very bright.

d) I put on my <u>shoes</u> (shoes, books) and went out
to play.

e) There was a large <u>spider</u> (drum, spider) in the web.

f) The <u>clock</u> (clock, hen) ticked very loudly.

KEEP iT UP

A dentist looks after my teeth

Remember

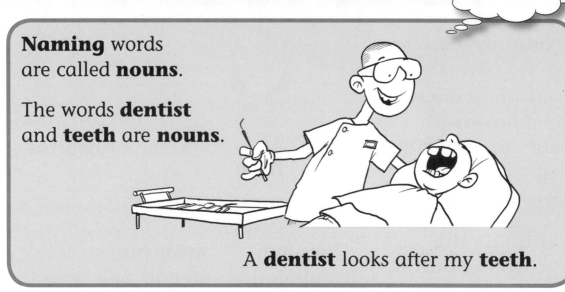

Naming words are called **nouns**.

The words **dentist** and **teeth** are **nouns**.

A **dentist** looks after my **teeth**.

1 **Choose the correct noun for each gap.**

 a) You shut a _____door_____. (door, apple)

 b) You sing a __song__. (cup, song)

 c) You climb a __ladder__. (book, ladder)

 d) You brush your __hair__. (face, hair)

 e) You kick a __ball__. (leg, ball)

 f) You dig with a __spade__. (spade, television)

2 **Think of a suitable noun for each sentence.**

 a) I wash my __body__.

 b) I dry myself with a __towel__.

 c) I clean my teeth with a __brush__.

 d) I wash my hair with __shampoo__.

 e) I turn on the __tap__.

 f) I fell off my __chair__.

 g) I made a __picter__ picture.

 h) I picked up a __bag__.

Fruit and vegetables

Remember

We can classify things in different sets.

sock   T-shirt   shorts   knife   fork   spoon

These are all **clothes**.   These are all **things we eat with**.

Write the names of these fruit and vegetables in the correct place.

orange   okra   potato   mango
callaloo   papaya   banana   cabbage
grape   carrot   sweetcorn   strawberry
pineapple   peas   melon   onion

names of fruit	names of vegetables
pineapple	carrot
grape	peas
orange	onions
melon	cabbage
banana	okra
strawberry	sweetcorn
mango	callaloo
papaya	potato

A survey

Remember

Carry out a survey.

Ask ten or more people what their favourite fruit and vegetables are.

Write down what they say.

A **survey** is when you want to find out some **information**. You **ask** people **questions** and **write** down their **answers**.

Name	Favourite fruit	Favourite vegetable
Scout	banana	cabbage
Neil	apple	carot
Roux	grape	cucumber
Xibbla	pepe vy s	peexeur
aveye	lopszta	z lool

Results

Write some sentences about what you have found out.

_____

_____

_____

Sets

Remember

We can **classify** things in **different sets**.
Socks, T-shirts and shorts are all **clothes**.
Knives, forks and spoons are all **things we eat with**.

1 Name these sets of nouns.

   a) cabbage, potato, carrot   They are all types
   of vegetables.

   b) tennis, cricket, swimming   *things for sports.*

   c) drums, piano, trumpet   *instruments*

   d) trousers, jacket, hat   *cloths*

   e) knife, fork, spoon   *Thigs We eat with.*

   f) car, bike, bus   *veakisvehicles.*

2 Underline the odd word out in each set.

a) mother	father	hen	sister
b) bean	bag	potato	pea
c) cup	apple	banana	orange
d) car	bike	bus	book
e) duck	sun	mouse	horse
f) pen	pencil	window	crayon
g) doctor	nurse	ball	dentist
h) house	cup	school	hospital
i) tree	shoe	boot	sneaker
j) sun	paper	star	moon

Remember

Some words often appear in **pairs**.

rice and peas   ackee and saltfish

Join the words that go together.   Write them here.

a) doctor   cart   ~~donkey cart~~

b) thunder   saucer   cup saucer

c) knife   ball   bat ball

d) cup   brush   comb brush

e) salt   nurse   doctor   nurse

f) bat   fork   fork spoon

g) donkey   pepper   pepper salt

h) paint   lightning   lightning thunder

i) hand   nail   nail hammer
                                     tree

j) bed   trunk

k) tree   mattress   bed mattress

l) flower   head   head hat

m) fire   stem   flower stem

n) hat   smoke   smoke fire

o) hammer   glove   hammer glove

34

Onions, peas, cabbage and sweetcorn

Remember

We use **commas** to **separate items in a list.**
We do not usually put a comma before the word **and** in a list.

My favourite vegetables are onions, peas, cabbage and sweetcorn.

1 **Write the missing commas in these lists.**

a) a tiger a zebra a camel and a lion

b) chicken beef pork and lamb

c) curry spaghetti sausages pizza and hamburgers

d) guitar drums trumpet and piano

e) one cat two dogs three hens and four goats

f) some cakes a can of cola a bar of chocolate and a bag of sweets

2 **Put in the missing commas in these sentences.**

a) On the road there were some buses lorries vans and cars.

b) For my birthday I had a ball a book a game and a jigsaw.

c) Sam got up dressed had his breakfast and went to school.

d) On the farm I saw a horse some cows some chickens and some sheep.

e) Anna has a round face black hair brown eyes and a small nose.

f) A hairdresser needs a brush a comb a mirror and some scissors.

Dangers in the kitchen

Look at this picture. Write some sentences about things you can see that could cause an accident.

Remember

Be careful! Many **accidents** happen in the **home**.

knife
iorn
pot

36

I rest, I am resting

Remember

A **verb** often tells us what someone or something is **doing**. The verb can be written in a **simple way**: The lion **sleeps**. The verb can be written a **longer way**: The lion **is sleeping**.

Fill in the charts correctly.

simple form of the verb		longer form of the verb	
I	rest	I	am resting
you	rest	you	are resting
he	rest	he	is resting
she	isresting	she	is resting
it	Isresting	it	Is resting
they	are resting	they	are resting

simple form of the verb		longer form of the verb	
I	eat	I	am eating
you	eat	you	are eating
he	eats	he	is eating
she	eats	she	Is eating
it	eats	it	Is eating
they	eats	they	are Eating

simple form of the verb		longer form of the verb	
I	play	I	am playing
you	playaying	you	are playing
he	plays	he	is playing
she	plays	she	is playing
it	plays	it	is playing
they	play	they	are playing

37

He is shouting

A **verb** tells us what someone or something is **doing**.

He **is shouting**.

1 Complete each sentence with the 'ing' form of the verb.

a) I am ___climbing___ (climb).

b) You are _shouting_ (shout).

c) He is _drawing_ (draw).

d) She is _singing_ (sing).

e) We are _laughing_ (laugh).

f) They are _playing_ (play).

g) It is _walking_ (walk).

h) It is _flying_ (fly).

i) She is _sleeping_ (sleep).

j) They are _drinking_ (drink).

2 Now write the short form of each sentence above.

a) I ___climb___ .   b) I am climbing

c) you climb   d) you are climbing

e) He is climbing   f) He is sing

g) She climb   h) She is cli

i) II climb   j) It is clio

38

Keeping fit

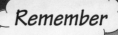

It is important to **exercise** and **keep fit**.

1   **Read the rhyme and do the actions to help you keep fit!**

Stand on your toes.
Blow your nose.
Bark like a dog.
Jump like a frog.
Thump your chest.
No time to rest!
Crawl on the floor.
Run to the door.
Put your hands in the air.
Open your eyes wide and stare.
Skip and hop.
Are you ready to drop?
Then it's time to STOP!

2   **Write about some things you can do to keep fit.**

Jump, hop, run, skiip
and stand on my toes.

Cross the road safely

Remember

It is important to **read** information **carefully**.

1 Read these road safety rules. They tell you how to cross a busy road safely.

1 Stop on the pavement, and stand still.	**2** Look both ways to see if any traffic is coming.
3 If something is coming, wait and let it go past you.	**4** Look and listen again.
5 When you are sure it is safe, walk straight across the road.	**6** Keep listening and looking while you are walking.

2 Draw a picture to go with each rule.

Keeping clean

It is important to **keep ourselves clean**!

There is something wrong with each sentence.
Rewrite each sentence so that it makes sense.

a) Take off your clothes and put them in the bath tub.

take off youre clotes and *the in the* putte me in the

b) Put the plug in the tap.

putt the Put the tap in the plug. *he*

c) Turn on the cold water and fill the bath.

turn on the warm wate r and fill the tub

d) Dive into the bath tub.

walk into the bath tub

e) Wash yourself well with toothpaste.

wash yourselfe werl with sope.

f) Lie back and relax under the water for a few hours.

Lie Back and rilax for *an Hour y*

g) Step out of the bath and turn on the light to let the water out.

stepout of the bath and turn on the ligt to let the wterout

h) Dry yourself on a wet towel.

Dry yourselfon a dry

i) Put on a nice set of dirty clothes.

putonaniceset of clien clotsete

41

Things we keep in the fridge

Remember

We use **commas** to **separate items in a list.**

We do **not** usually put a comma before the word **and** in a list.

We keep milk, cheese, yogurt and eggs in the fridge.

Complete these sentences in your own words.
Remember the commas.

a) Four things I like to eat are eggs, Yogurt, rasin bread bananas.

b) Five things I can see out of my bedroom window are birdhouse, flowerpot fence l bug hotel butterfly,

c) In the fridge at home we keep milk carrot c

d) The names of five children in my class are coko Miles Finn Elliot mason.

e) Some things you can buy at a supermarket are eggs fish meat

f) The colours of the rainbow are red, green, blue

g) The days of the week are sunday Monday Friday

h) The names of some trees are oak ash mapale

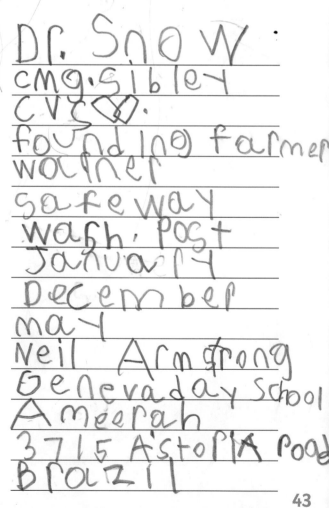

Remember

A **proper noun** is the name of a **particular person**, **place** or **thing**. A proper noun always **begins** with a **capital letter**.

My name is **Doctor Brown**. I work in **Mandeville Hospital**.

Write some proper nouns. Remember to begin each one with a capital letter.

Write the name of:

a) a doctor you know — Dr. Snow

b) a hospital near you — cmg.sibley

c) a chemist near you — CVS.

d) a restaurant near you — founding farmer

e) a church near you — warner

f) a supermarket near you — safeway

g) a newspaper — wash. Post

h) the first month of the year — January

i) the last month of the year — December

j) the fifth month of the year — may

k) someone famous — Neil Armstrong

l) your school — Geneva day School

m) a good friend — Ameerah

n) the place you live — 3715 Astoria road

o) a country beginning with B — Brazil

Remember

It is important to **eat healthy food**.

Make up a menu for one day with food which is healthy and good for you. Remember to say what you will drink, too.

Breakfast

ham sandwich
strawberry juice

Lunch
fish banana
water

pizza

Dinner
orange
water

Remember

It is important to get plenty of **sleep**.

1 **Read this rhyme.**

Go to bed
Go to bed early – wake up with joy;
Go to bed late – cross girl or boy.
Go to bed early – ready for play;
Go to bed late – tired all day.

Go to bed early – no pains or ills;
Go to bed late – doctors and pills.
Go to bed early – grow very tall;
Go to bed late – stay very small.

2 **Write some sentences.**
Say what you can learn from the rhyme.

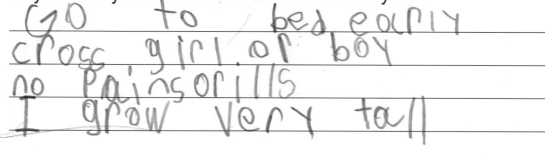

Go to bed early
cross girl or boy
no pains or ills
I grow very tall

Remember

Sometimes we can just add '**ing**' to a verb and it does **not** change the spelling of the **root** verb.

climb – climbing

Sometimes when we add '**ing**' it **changes** the spelling of the root verb.

bake – baking   swim – swimming

1 **Complete the charts correctly. Add 'ing' to each verb.**

bark	barking	like	liking	hop	hopping
jump	jumping	close	closing	pat	patting
lick	licking	hope	hoping	jog	jogging
look	looking	phone	phoning	tap	tapping
brush	brushing	bake	baking	hug	hugging
kick	kicking	wave	waving	clap	clapping

2 **Take 'ing' off each verb. Write the short form of the verb. Take care with your spelling!**

a) acting __, act__   b) bending __bend__

c) biting __bite__   d) diving __dive__

e) begging __beg__   f) running __run__

g) dancing __dance__   h) combing __comb__

i) digging __dig__   j) giving __give__

k) writing __write__   l) lifting __lift__

m) planting __plant__   n) shaking __shake__

o) skipping __skip__

The accident

Remember

You can write a **report** to tell people about personal experiences.

Have you ever had an accident?
Write about it.

Explain:

- where you were.
- how the accident happened.
- how you hurt yourself.
- what you have learnt from your experience.

- who helped you.
- what they did.
- how you felt.

Test 1

1 Write these words in alphabetical order:
spider   ant   crocodile _ant_   _crocodile_ _spider_

2 Underline the common word that contains a 'hen'.
where   what   <u>when</u>   why

3 There are no spaces between the words in this sentence.
Write it and punctuate it correctly.
myheadisonmyneck _my head is on_
my neke

4 Complete the sentence correctly.
_I_ (I, Me) have a mouth.

5 Choose the correct word to complete the sentence.
This book is _mine_ (my, mine).

6 Underline the verb in this sentence:
A frog <u>hops</u> into a pond.

7 Underline the noun in this sentence:
I write with a <u>pencil</u>.

8 Choose 'a' or 'an' to complete this phrase:
_an_ orange

9 Write the plural:
one goat but two _goats_

10 Write the singular:
one _glase_ but two glasses

11 Underline the adjective in this sentence:
The girl had a <u>fizzy</u> drink.

48

Test 1

12 Choose the correct form of adjective to complete the sentence.

Colin is _taller_ (taller, tallest) than me. ☐

13 Begin the proper noun in this sentence with a capital letter.

The plane landed in london. _the plane_ ☐

landed in london

14 Underline the opposite of 'wet'. ☐

dirty   <u>dry</u>   dear

15 Underline the odd noun out in this set: ☐

brother   grandmother   <u>bird</u>   aunt

16 Choose the best word to complete this phrase: ☐

knife and _fork_ (fish, fork, four)

17 Put in the missing commas in this sentence: ☐

My favourite colours are red, yellow, green, and blue.

18 Choose the best word to complete the sentence. ☐

The boy sits in a chair and _he_ (he, she) reads a book.

19 Write the name of your country: _usa_ ☐

20 Write and punctuate this sentence correctly. ☐

a fish swims in the sea _A fish swims in_

the sea.

Scoring:
Each question is worth 1 mark.   Complete this:
Mark your test.   **I scored _20_ out of 20.**

49

Family words

Remember

There are **five vowels**.
They are:

a e i o u

Every word must contain **at least one** vowel.
Sometimes the letter **y** acts as a **part-time vowel**
(e.g. family).

Read the meaning of each word.
Then fill in the missing vowels in the words.

a) f a m i l y — parents and their children and grandchildren

b) f r i e n d — someone you like and who likes you

c) r e l a t i v e — someone in the same family as you

d) n e i g h b o u r — someone who lives next door or near to you

e) p a r e n t — a person who has a child

f) b e h a v e o u r — how you behave

g) c o o p e r a t e — to work together

h) d u t y — what you should do

i) r e s p o n s e b l e — being in charge of doing something

j) v a l u e s — things you believe are important

Alphabetical order

Remember

These words are in **alphabetical order**, according to their **first** letters:

brother   **f**ather   **m**other

These words are in **alphabetical order**, according to their **second** letters:

b**a**th   b**e**d   b**r**other

1 Write these words in alphabetical order, according to their first letters.

a) parent   family   neighbour   visitor
   family   *neighbour*   *parent*   *visitor*

b) leader   group   relative.   school
   group   *leader*   *relative*   *school*

c) event   hero   activity   politeness
   activity   *event*   *hero*   *politeness*

d) farmer   teacher   doctor   engineer
   doctor   *engineer*   *farmer*   *teacher*

2 Write these words in alphabetical order, according to their second letters.

a) community   celebration   chore
   celebration   *chore*   *community*

b) holiday   history   husband
   history   *holiday*   *husband*

c) social   share   style
   share   *social*   *style*

d) friend   fisherman   flag
   fisherman   *flag*   *friend*

51

Verb families

We belong to a family.
All **verbs** belong to a **family**, too.

Family name	Verbs in the family
to play	play
	plays
	playing
	played

cooking   walks   paint   paints   cook   walked
painting   cooked   walk   painted   cooks   walking

Fill in each verb from the box in the correct verb family in the chart.

to paint	to cook	to walk
paint	cook	walks
painted	cooked	walks
paints	cooking	walking
painting	cooks	walked

52

Yesterday I celebrated my birthday

Remember

Sometimes a verb tells you what happened **in the past**. These verbs often **end** in '**ed**'.

Yesterday I **celebrated** my birthday.

1 **Underline the verb in each sentence.**

a) The child <u>knocked</u> on the door.

b) The girl opened her present.

c) The boy jumped with joy.

d) The children danced to the music.

e) The man washed his hands.

f) I walked over the bridge.

2 **Add 'ed' to the end of each verb.**

a) Yesterday I _____ (kick) a ball.

b) Yesterday I _____ (cook) an egg.

c) Yesterday I _____ (open) a door.

d) Yesterday I _____ (play) with a friend.

e) Yesterday I _____ (walk) to town.

f) Yesterday I _____ (brush) my teeth.

3 **Write a sentence about something you did yesterday. Underline the verb in it.**

_____

Who is your best friend?

Remember

We ask **questions** to **find things out**.
A question **begins** with a **capital letter.**
A question **ends** with a **question mark**.

Are you going home now?

Write these questions correctly.

a) who is your best friend

_____

b) is the sun hot

_____

c) what is your favourite colour

_____

d) is this the way to Spanish Town

_____

e) is it raining

_____

f) are you going to school today

_____

g) are the cows brown or black

_____

h) are your grandparents kind to you

_____

i) what day is it tomorrow

_____

j) do you like going on a picnic

_____

Remember

> We ask **questions** to **find things out**.
> A question **begins** with a **capital letter**.
> A question **ends** with a **question mark**.

1 Choose the best word from the box to begin each question.

2 Write the question marks at the end of the questions.

3 Write an answer for each question.

> Who   What   Where   Why   When

a) _____ is the time __

_____

b) _____ is your school __

_____

c) _____ are your best friends __

_____

d) _____ is your birthday __

_____

e) _____ are families important __

_____

4 Make up a 'Who', 'What', 'Where', 'When' or 'Why' question of your own.

_____

Can you see the sea?

Some words **sound the same** but are **spelled differently** and have **different meanings**.

I can **see** the **sea**.

1 **Match the words that sound the same.**

Write them here.

see	weight
right	waist
wait	sea
waste	steal
steel	write
hear	their
there	sun
son	here

_____

_____

<u>see</u>   <u>sea</u>

_____

_____

_____

_____

_____

2 **Choose the correct word for each sentence.**

a) You swim in the _____ (see, sea).

b) You _____ (write, right) a story.

c) Scales tell you your _____ (wait, weight).

d) It is wrong to _____ (waist, waste) things.

e) It is wrong to _____ (steal, steel) things.

f) I can _____ (here, hear) a noise.

g) The _____ (son, sun) is shining.

h) The children took _____ (there, their) books home.

56

The grass is green

The verb **to be** is a **being** verb.

It tells us what someone or something **is**.

Grass **is** green.   The children **are** happy.

Here are the parts of the verb 'to be'.

It is important to learn them.

I am   you are   he is   she is   it is   we are   they are

1 **Choose the correct form of the verb for each sentence.**

   a) I _____ (am/are) at school.

   b) It _____ (is/are) my birthday today.

   c) My parents look after me. They _____ (is/are) kind.

   d) You _____ (am/are) good at cooking.

   e) We _____ (is/are) at home.

2 **Write these sentences correctly.**

   a) My mum works hard. She are busy all day.

   _____

   b) My dad likes shopping. He am at the supermarket.

   _____

   c) We is members of a family.

   _____

   d) I are very happy.

   _____

   e) The children like school. They am good children.

   _____

A smart uniform

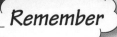
An **adjective** is a **describing** word.

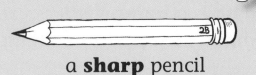

a **sharp** pencil

1 **Underline the adjective in each phrase.**

a) a sharp pencil   **b)** an interesting book

c) a noisy child   **d)** a hot lunch

e) a difficult word   **f)** a good song

g) a cold drink   **h)** a best friend

i) a smart uniform   **j)** a tall building

k) an empty bin   **l)** an open window

2 **Choose the best adjective for each gap.**

a) a _____ (loud, windy) voice

b) a _____ (busy, funny) playground

c) a _____ (soft, heavy) rock

d) some _____ (black, green) grass

e) a _____ (straight, fast) car

f) three _____ (deep, naughty) monkeys

g) a _____ (wet, long) story

h) an _____ (empty, open) glass

i) a _____ (wooden, brave) desk

j) a _____ (wild, steep) hill

happy/unhappy; agree/disagree

Remember

We can add '**un**' and '**dis**' to the **beginning** of some words.
They give the word the **opposite** meaning.

  happy   **un**happy    agree   **dis**agree

1 Make the words.

a) un + happy = ___unhappy___

b) un + well = _____

c) un + fair = _____

d) un + kind = _____

e) dis + agree = _____

f) dis + obey = _____

g) dis + trust = _____

h) dis + honest = _____

2 Write the words that mean the opposite of these words.

a) unwell ___well___   **b)** disagree _____

c) disobey _____   **d)** unhappy _____

e) unfair _____   **f)** unkind _____

g) distrust _____   **h)** dishonest _____

3 Write a sentence about something that is unfair.

_____

4 Write a sentence about something you disagree with.

_____

Jumped, skipped and waved

Remember

Sometimes we can just add '**ed**' to a verb and it does **not** change the spelling of the **root** verb.

bark – barked

Sometimes when we add '**ed**' it **changes** the spelling of the root verb.

like – liked   hop – hopped

Complete the charts correctly.
Add 'ed' to each verb.

1

bark	barked
jump	
lick	
look	
brush	
kick	

2

like	liked
close	
hope	
phone	
bake	
wave	

3

hop	hopped
pat	
jog	
tap	
hug	
skip	

1 Read this poem.

Remember

Families are very **important**.

Some places I visited

I visited my friend's house
My friends were singing.
They really enjoyed singing.
I smiled when I saw them singing.

I visited my school
The teachers were teaching.
They really enjoyed teaching.
I smiled when I saw them teaching.

I visited my classroom
The children were working.
They really enjoyed working.
I smiled when I saw them working.

I visited a hospital
The nurses were nursing.
They really enjoyed nursing.
I smiled when I saw them nursing.

I visited a farm
The farmers were farming.
They really enjoyed farming.
I smiled when I saw them farming.

I came back home
My parents were laughing.
They really enjoyed laughing.
I smiled when I saw them laughing.

2 **Write something you can learn from the poem.**

_____

_____

Remember

Here are the parts of the verb **to be** in the **present tense**. It is important to **learn** them.

I am	he is	she is	it is
we are	you are	they are	

1 **Choose 'am', 'is' or 'are' to complete each sentence.**

a) My house is in Montego Bay. It _____ nice here.

b) My mum and dad grow vegetables. They _____ in the garden.

c) I _____ awake.

d) You _____ a good friend.

e) We _____ sad sometimes.

f) I go to a big school. It _____ near my house.

g) My sister swims well. She _____ in the school team.

2 **The underlined verb is wrong in each sentence. Write each sentence correctly.**

a) You <u>is</u> like your mother.   _____

b) I <u>are</u> very tired.   _____

c) We <u>is</u> nice to our friends.   _____

d) They <u>am</u> my grandparents.   _____

e) It <u>are</u> a fine day today.   _____

f) She <u>am</u> a good reader.   _____

g) He <u>are</u> my neighbour.   _____

My aunt is eating an apple

Remember

Sometimes a verb is made up of **two words**.

My aunt **is eating** an apple.

1 Choose 'am', 'is' or 'are' to complete the verb in each sentence.

   a) He _____ running.   **b)** I _____ laughing.

   c) She _____ cooking.   **d)** They _____ jumping.

   e) It _____ building a nest.

   f) We _____ smiling.

   g) You _____ digging the garden.

   h) We go to church every Sunday. We _____ going to church today.

2 Write these sentences correctly.

   a) I are watching cricket on TV.

   _____

   b) It am raining.

   _____

   c) You is helping me with my spelling.

   _____

   d) My friends is playing outside.

   _____

   e) I are waiting for my birthday.

   _____

   f) We am going on holiday soon.

   _____

Behaving correctly

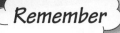

We should **behave in the right way** at all times.

1 Read the list. Some of these things are right. They are what we should do. Some of these things are bad. We should not do them.

- to bully
- to share
- to help others
- to lie
- to say 'please' and 'thank you'
- to cheat
- to think of other people's feelings
- to steal

- to say nasty things
- to spend time with your friends
- to hurt people
- to be selfish
- to be nice to members of your family
- to show your parents you are grateful for what they do for you

2 Now write each thing in the chart in the correct place.

Good behaviour	Bad behaviour

Have you got any brothers or sisters?

Remember

We ask **questions** to **find things out**.
We can use the verb **to have** to ask questions.

1 Choose 'Has' or 'Have' to begin each question.

2 Finish each question with a question mark.

3 Write an answer for each question.

a) _____ you got any brothers or sisters__

_____

b) _____ your mother got a red dress__

_____

c) _____ your school got a lot of children__

_____

d) _____ you got any homework __

_____

e) _____ your house got a front door__

_____

f) _____ your shoes got laces__

_____

g) _____ your teacher got a car__

_____

h) _____ you got any neighbours__

_____

Things people do to help me at home

There are **lots of jobs** that need doing **in a home**.

1   Make a list of things different people do to help you at home.

2   Make a list of some things you can do to help at home.

Saying 'Thank-you'

Remember

It is important to say '**please**' and '**thank-you**'.

Make a thank-you card for someone who helps you.

Dear _____

I want to say a big

thank you

for helping me.

Love from _____

I was, you were

Here are the parts of the verb **to be** in the **past tense**.
It is important to **learn** them.

I was	he was	she was	it was
we were	you were	they were	

1 **Choose the correct form of the verb for each sentence.**

a) I _____ (was/were) very cold.

b) My dog barked. It _____ (was/were) hungry.

c) My aunt and uncle came to my party. They _____ (was/were) nice.

d) You _____ (was/were) very brave when you hurt yourself.

e) We _____ (was/were) quite noisy at the party.

2 **Write each sentence correctly.**

a) My grandma worked hard. She were busy all day.

_____

b) When my grandpa dug up some vegetables he were tired.

_____

c) I were sorry when it were time to go.

_____

d) We was late for school yesterday.

_____

e) When my brother sang a song he were very noisy.

_____

They and them

When I talk **about more than one person or thing**, I use the words **they** or **them**.

The children were very noisy.
They were shouting.
Everyone was looking at **them**.

1 **Choose 'they' or 'them' to complete the sentences.**

a) There are lots of teachers at my school. _____ are all very nice.

b) My parents look after me. I love _____ very much.

c) Anna and Sam ran home. _____ were late.

d) Uncle John and Aunt Jane came last week. I gave _____ a big hug.

e) Mice squeak. _____ have long tails.

2 **Write these sentences correctly.**

a) I love reading books when them are interesting.

_____

b) I had lots of birthday cards. I put they all on the shelf.

_____

c) The bees were buzzing as them flew along.

_____

d) Some birds lay eggs and then them sit on they.

_____

e) When my friends come to play them bring some toys with they.

_____

When I was ill

It is good to write about our **personal experiences.**

Remember

Write about a time when you were ill.

Before you write, think about these questions:

- What was the matter with you?
- Did you go to see a doctor?
- Did a doctor come to see you?
- Did you have to stay at home?
- Did you have to stay in bed?
- Did you need any medicine?
- Who looked after you?
- How long were you ill?

Do you like singing?

Remember

We ask **questions** to **find things out**.
We can use the verb **to do** to ask questions.

1   Choose 'Do' or 'Does' to begin each question.

2   Finish each question with a question mark.

3   Write an answer for each question.

a) _____ you like singing__

_____

b) _____ your family have any pets__

_____

c) _____ your class go on any visits__

_____

d) _____ you read a lot__

_____

e) _____ your friends come to your house to play__

_____

f) _____ your teacher help you at school__

_____

g) _____ you think it is right to tell lies__

_____

h) _____ a cat have fur__

_____

House rules

Remember

Rules are important. A rule is something that **tells us what we should do**.

Look at this poster. It is a set of five rules for a pet cat!

Rules for Cats

- No scratching

- No chasing birds

- No fighting with the dog

- No howling at night

- No jumping on the kitchen table

Make up five house rules for children. Draw a picture.

House Rules for Children

- _____

- _____

- _____

- _____

- _____

Verb families

Remember

All verbs belong to a **family.**

verb family name – to play
verbs in the family – play, plays, playing, played

Complete each family of verbs. Some are done for you.

Family name	Verb with **no** ending	Verb with 's' ending	Verb with **'ing'** ending	Verb with **'ed'** ending
to bang	bang	bangs	banging	banged
to talk			talking	
to shout		shouts		
to pull				pulled
to push		pushes		
to open			opening	
to mix				
to colour				
to bake				
to skip				
to laugh				
to splash				
to lift				
to wash				

Read the meaning of each word.

Then fill in the missing vowels in the words.

Remember

There are **five vowels.**
They are:

      a   e   i   o   u

Every word must contain **at least one** vowel.
Sometimes the letter **y** acts as a **part-time vowel** (e.g. stud**y**).

a) s c h _ _ l   a place we go to learn

b) t _ r m   each school year is divided into three of these

c) s t _ d _   to learn about something

d) t r _ v _ l   to move from one place to another

e) t r _ f f _ c   cars, trucks, buses and other things travelling on the road

f) j _ b   what people do to earn a living

g) s k _ l l   the ability to do something well

h) r _ l _ x   to rest

i) h _ b b _   something interesting you do in your spare time

j) w _ _ t h _ r   this may be sunny, rainy or windy

Brother, father, mother

Remember

These words are in **alphabetical order,** according to
their **first** letters: **b**rother **f**ather **m**other
These words all **begin** with the **same** letter.
They are in alphabetical order, according to their **second**
letters: b**a**th   b**e**d   b**r**other

1 Write these words in alphabetical order, according
to their first letters.

a) term   job   relax   hobby

_____   _____   _____   _____

b) college   brain   delay   ambulance

_____   _____   _____   _____

c) vehicle   computer   leisure   airport

_____   _____   _____   _____

2 Write these words in alphabetical order, according
to their second letters.

a) skill   study   school

_____   _____   _____

b) travel   term   ticket

_____   _____   _____

c) weather   work   where

_____   _____   _____

I think a rest is best!

Remember

Learning to **rhyme** helps with spelling.

I think a **rest** in my **nest** is **best**!

Make some new words.

1 Change the 'r' in 'rest' to:

b ___best___   n _____   p _____

t _____   v _____   w _____

ch _____

2 Change the 'sl' in 'sleep' to:

cr _____   d _____   k _____

p _____   w _____   bl _____

3 Change the 'b' in 'bed' to:

f _____   l _____   r _____

w _____   bl _____   fl _____

sh _____

4 Change the 'sn' in 'snore' to:

b _____   c _____   m _____

s _____   w _____   sh _____

5 Think of as many words as possible that rhyme with 'well'.

She was a good teacher

When we use the verb **to be**, we use **was** or **were** in the past tense.

1 Choose 'was' or 'were' to complete each sentence.

a) The sun shone brightly. It _____ hot.

b) My mum and dad _____ married a long time ago.

c) I _____ awake during the thunderstorm.

d) You _____ a good friend when you helped me with my homework.

e) We _____ sad when our pet died.

f) The mango looked ripe. It _____ very juicy.

g) Yesterday my sister _____ ill.

2 The underlined verb is wrong in each sentence. Write each sentence correctly.

a) You <u>was</u> last in the race. _____

b) I <u>were</u> very thirsty. _____

c) We <u>was</u> good friends. _____

d) They <u>was</u> very hot. _____

e) It <u>were</u> a fine day yesterday. _____

f) She <u>were</u> a good teacher. _____

g) He <u>were</u> in the school team. _____

He or him, she or her

When I talk **about** another male, I use the words **he**
or **him**. When I talk **about** another female, I use the
words **she** or **her**.

John is a nice boy. I like **him**. **He** is in my class.
Anna is a nice girl. I like **her**. **She** is a good friend.

1 **Choose the correct word to complete each sentence.**

a) My father works every day. _____ (He, She) gets up
very early.

b) My mother is a good cook. _____ (He, She) makes
lovely cakes.

c) My aunt has a car. I saw _____ (him, her) in it.

d) My uncle has a dog. The dog loves _____ (him, her).

e) The boy ran quickly. _____ (He, She) was a good
runner.

f) My grandmother loves _____ (his, her) flower
garden.

2 **Write these sentences correctly.**

a) When the girl sat down he read a book.

_____

b) The old lady was tired so I helped him with his
shopping.

_____

c) The old man smiled when I told her a joke.

_____

d) My teacher's name is Mr Jones. She is very nice.

_____

I rode my bicycle

Remember

We cannot add '**ed**' to the **end** of some **verbs** to make the **past tense**.
These verbs are called **irregular verbs**.
Yesterday I ~~rided~~ **rode** my bicycle.

1 **Match the present tense of each verb with its past tense.**

Write them here.

present tense	past tense	
a) I ride	I broke	_____
b) I go	I rode	I ride I rode
c) I make	I saw	_____
d) I see	I ate	_____
e) I break	I went	_____
f) I eat	I made	_____
g) I catch	I wrote	_____
h) I write	I caught	_____

2 **Rewrite each sentence in the past tense.**

a) I go to school.　　_____

b) I eat my lunch.　　_____

c) I catch a ball.　　_____

d) I break my toy.　　_____

e) I ride my bike.　　_____

f) I make a mistake.　　_____

g) I see my friend.　　_____

Recording personal information

Sometimes we need to **record personal information** and to **give our opinion** on things.

Complete the information in the chart.

My school

My school is called _____

My school's address is _____

_____

My school begins at _____ each day.

My school ends at _____ each day.

I like my school because _____

_____

The Principal's name is _____

My school has _____ classes.

My teacher's name is _____

My class has _____ children in it.

I go to school to learn to _____

_____

Tick which of these subjects you like:

reading ☐   writing ☐   spelling ☐

maths ☐   history ☐   geography ☐

art ☐   PE ☐   music ☐

My favourite subject is _____

I like it because _____

_____

My first day at school

Remember

It is good to write about our **personal experiences.**

Write about your first day at school.

Say:

- how old you were
- who took you to school
- how you felt
- who your teacher was
- which school you went to
- what happened

My first day at school

_____

_____

_____

_____

_____

_____

People, places and things

Naming words are called **nouns**.
A noun may be the name of a **person**, **place** or **thing**.

bus

school

girl

The **girl** went to **school** on a **bus**.

The word **girl** is the name of a **person**.
The word **school** is the name of a **place**.
The word **bus** is the name of a **thing**.

Write these nouns in the correct place on the chart.

teacher	chair	doctor	book	pencil
boy	hammer	girl	factory	shop
optician	tree	drum	hotel	library
hairdresser	airport	bus	driver	garage
plane	school	hospital	builder	

names of people	names of places	names of things

One baby, lots of babies

A noun may be **singular** or **plural**.
Singular means **one** thing.
Plural means **more than one** thing.

one baby

We change the '**y**' to '**i**' and add '**es**' to make the singular noun **baby** into the plural noun **babies**.

lots of babies

1   Fill in the missing plural nouns.

    a) one lady   two _____

    b) one factory   two _____

    c) one baby   two _____

    d) one puppy   two _____

    e) one copy   two _____

    f) one hobby   two _____

    g) one fly   two _____

    h) one try   two _____

2   Fill in the missing singular nouns.

    a) one _____ two cities

    b) one _____ two stories

    c) one _____ two berries

    d) one _____ two diaries

    e) one _____ two injuries

    f) one _____ two ponies

    g) one _____ two butterflies

    h) one _____ two cherries

I went to school

Remember

You cannot add '**ed**' to **irregular verbs** to make the **past tense.**
(verb: to go) Yesterday I ~~goed~~ **went** to school.

1 Choose the correct form of the past tense for each sentence.

   a) The boy _____ (breaked/broke) the window.

   b) Yesterday I _____ (goed/went) to a party.

   c) My teacher _____ (teached/taught) me how to read.

   d) I _____ (seed/saw) my friend at school.

   e) We _____ (maked/made) a loud noise.

   f) I _____ (writed/wrote) a 'thank-you' letter to my uncle.

2 Write each sentence as if it happened yesterday.

Present tense	Past tense
a) I feel ill.	Yesterday I felt ill.
b) I ride a horse.	_____
c) I eat an apple.	_____
d) I sing a song.	_____
e) I catch a ball.	_____
f) I go to school.	_____

School sounds

Remember

Listening is an important skill.

1 **What sounds do you hear in your school? Read this poem.**

School sounds

Pencils writing, children wriggling,
People laughing, children giggling,
Crayons drawing, pencils scribbling,
Teachers talking, children dribbling.

Paper folding, paper ripping,
Footsteps running, footsteps tripping,
Paper for writing, paper for spelling,
Noisy voices, shouting and yelling.

Doors shutting, doors banging,
Bells ringing, bells clanging,
Secret messages, secret notes,
Pick up bags, put on coats.

Ball bouncing, hands clapping,
Skipping ropes, slap, slap, slapping,
Voices quiet, voices loud,
Voices heard above the crowd.

Clock ticking on the wall,
Hands of clock seem to crawl,
Clock ticking far too slow,
Teacher, teacher, it's time to go!

2 **What sounds can you hear in your school? Make a list.**

Leisure time survey

Remember

1 Carry out a survey.

Ask ten or more people how they spend their leisure time.

> A **survey** is when you want to **find out** some **information**. You **ask people questions** and **write down their answers**.

Tick what they do on your chart.

Write down anything else that is not on your chart.

Name	Read	Watch TV	Play sport	Play on computer	Play music	Play with friends	Something else

2 Results.

Write some sentences about what you have found out.

_____

_____

_____

_____

_____

Remember

> **Play** and **relaxation** are important, but it is important to **play safely** at all times.

1 Read these hints for playing safely.
   Think of a sensible word for each gap.

Handy Hints for playing safely!

- Broken glass and rusty tins can _____ you.
- Never try to eat or _____ anything you find on the ground.
- Never _____ with fire.
- If you play with fire you could get _____.
- Never play _____ electricity.
- If you cannot swim, don't play near _____.
- Be careful! The water in ponds and lakes can be very _____.
- In rivers and the sea, the water can be very _____.
- Sometimes you cannot _____ what is in the water.
- Some people dump rubbish and broken _____ in the sea.

Remember

We can **classify** things in **different sets**.

sock

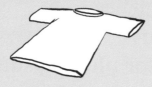
T-shirt

shorts

These are all **clothes**.

Below are the names of different types of transport.
Write each thing in the correct place on the chart.

yacht	truck	rowing boat	van	canoe
plane	helicopter	glider	bus	liner
taxi	rocket	sailing boat	car	bicycle
submarine	motor cycle	hot-air balloon	jet	coach

Things which go:		
in the water	on land	in the air

88

Sunshine at the seaside

Remember

We can sometimes put **two words together** to make **one new word**.

sea + side = seaside

1 **Do these word sums.**

 a) sun   + shine = _____

 b) bath + room   = _____

 c) farm + yard   = _____

 d) pan   + cake   = _____

 e) butter + fly   = _____

 f) birth + day   = _____

 g) book   + case   = _____

 h) water + fall   = _____

2 **Write some sentences. Use each word in a sentence.**

_____

_____

_____

_____

_____

_____

_____

You and your

When I talk to **another person**, I use the words **you** and **your**.

Hello. How are **you**? I like **your** cap.

1 Write the correct word in each gap.

a) When _____ (you, your) run, _____ (you, your) heart beats fast.

b) Did _____ (you, your) know, _____ (you, your) have more than 200 bones in _____ (you, your) body?

c) _____ (You, Your) brain helps _____ (you, your) to think.

d) Where are _____ (you, your) going?

e) Can _____ (you, your) please pass me _____ (you, your) pencil?

2 Write each sentence correctly.

a) Your have got a very nice house.

_____

b) I think you picture looks very nice.

_____

c) Will your take me to see you aunt?

_____

d) Your must never tell lies.

_____

e) I would like to be you friend.

_____

Be careful!

Remember

When we add **full** to the end of a word to make an **adjective** we only use **one** 'l' (**ful**).

care – care**ful**

1 Read the words.

> useful   careful   hopeful   powerful   painful
>
> cheerful   helpful   restful   thankful   colourful

2 Write the word that means full of:

a) colour   colourful   **b)** help   _____

c) use   _____   **d)** care   _____

e) rest   _____   **f)** pain   _____

g) cheer   _____   **h)** hope   _____

i) power   _____   **j)** thanks   _____

3 Choose five 'ful' adjectives.
   Make up some sentences and use the words in them.

_____

_____

_____

_____

_____

Types of sport

It is important to **play sport** and **keep fit**.

Match the sports with the pictures.

swimming football tennis basketball fishing
pool boxing cricket rollerblading

 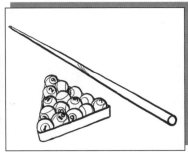 

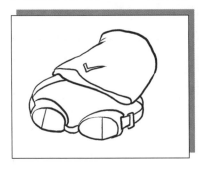  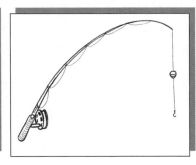

Broken bones

It is important to **play sport** and **keep fit** but you have to be careful!

Remember

Your friend Pam is in hospital! She fell over and broke her leg in a running race. You go to visit her.

1 You are allowed to take her *five* things.

2 Choose *five* things from the list.

3 Write your reason for choosing each thing.

✓	I would take	Reason
	some books to read	
	a radio	
	some fruit	
	a game to play	
	some orange juice	
	some clothes	
	a photo of her friends	
	some flowers	
	a 'Get Well Soon' card	
	a clock or watch	
	some pencils and crayons	
	some writing paper	

Test 2

1 Choose the correct form of the verb to complete this sentence:

My brother _____ (is, are) washing his hands.

2 Write this sentence in the past tense:

I call for my friend. _____

3 Write this question and punctuate it correctly:

where do you live _____

4 Choose the correct word to complete this sentence:

It is very nice _____ (hear, here).

5 Choose the best pronoun to complete this sentence:

_____ (I, She) runs fast.

6 Underline the adjective in this sentence:

The man put his empty glass on the table.

7 Choose 'un' or 'dis' to complete this word:

_____ appear

8 Add 'ed' to the end of this verb and change it to the past tense. Take care with the spelling!

stop _____

9 Write the correct form of the verb in this sentence:

The children are _____ (eat) sandwiches.

10 Complete this sentence with 'has' or 'have':

My mum _____ got brown eyes.

Test 2

11 Choose 'they' or 'them' to complete this sentence:
The girls took their bags home with _____.

12 Choose 'do' or 'does' to complete this sentence:
My television _____ not work.

13 Underline the word that rhymes with 'seat':
great   sweat   heat

14 Rewrite this sentence correctly.
My grandmother wears she glasses when her reads.

_____

15 Underline the past tense of the verb 'to go':
going   was   went

16 Write the plural of this word:
lady   _____

17 Underline the three tools in this group of nouns:
hammer   apple   saw   clock   bus   screwdriver

18 Choose the best ending for this compound word:
sun_____ (drop, shine)

19 Rewrite this sentence correctly.
Have your got you lunch in that bag?

_____

20 Underline the word that is spelled incorrectly in this sentence:
The sunset was wonderfull.

Scoring:
Each question is worth 1 mark.   Complete this:
Mark your test.   **I scored ____ out of 20.**

Community words

There are **five vowels**.
They are:

a   e   i   o   u

Every word must contain **at least one** vowel.
Sometimes the letter **y** acts as a **part-time vowel**
(e.g. family).

Read the meaning of each word.
Then fill in the missing vowels in the words.

a) f _ r m _ r   someone who works on a farm

b) f _ s h _ r m _ n   someone who catches fish

c) b _ _ l d _ r   someone who builds houses

d) f _ c t _ r _   a place where things are made

e) t _ w n   a place with lots of houses and shops

f) v _ l l _ g _   a small town in the country

g) m _ _ n t _ _ n   a very high hill

h) v _ l l _ y   low land between hills

i) l _ k _   a large area of water with land around it

j) p _ n d   a very small lake

Sorting the words out

These words are in **alphabetical order**, according to their **first** letters:

brother **f**ather **m**other

These words all begin with the **same** letter.
They are in **alphabetical order**, according to their **second** letters:

b**a**th b**e**d b**r**other

1 Write these words in alphabetical order, according to their first letters.

a) mountain   valley   hill   lake

_____   _____   _____   _____

b) concrete   brick   stone   marble

_____   _____   _____   _____

c) old   modern   new   ancient

_____   _____   _____

2 Write these words in alphabetical order, according to their second letters.

a) fisherman   ferry   farmer   flag

_____   _____   _____   _____

b) builder   bridge   barn   beach

_____   _____   _____   _____

c) city   community   church   cave

_____   _____   _____   _____

A builder builds

Remember

The letters 'er' often come at the **end** of a word.
These words often mean **someone
who does something.**
These words are all **nouns**.
A build**er** builds houses.

1 Write these 'er' words in alphabetical order.

a) teacher   gardener   cleaner   builder   painter

_____   _____   _____   _____   _____

b) reporter   driver   baker   butcher   plumber

_____   _____   _____   _____   _____

2 Write the name of a person who:

a) builds   _____   **b)** paints   _____

c) bakes bread _____   **d)** drives trucks _____

e) cleans   _____   **f)** reports the
news   _____

g) teaches   _____   **h)** gardens   _____

i) sells meat   _____   **j)** does plumbing _____

3 Write some sentences. Use some of the 'er' words
above in them.

_____

_____

_____

_____

_____

People who keep us safe – the fireman

Remember

In our community there
are lots of people **who keep us safe**.

Complete these sentences correctly.

a) This is a _____ (policeman, fireman).

b) A fireman fights _____ (fires, people).

c) A fireman is very _____ (brave, slow).

d) A fireman uses _____ (ice, water) to put out fires.

e) A fireman keeps us _____ (indoors, safe).

f) A fireman wears a _____ (dress, uniform).

g) A fireman wears a _____ (helmet, hammer) on
his head.

h) A fireman drives a special _____ (train, truck).

i) The fire truck has a _____ (leader, ladder) on it.

j) The fire truck makes a _____ (loud, long) noise to
warn people to get out of the way.

Remember

In our community there are lots of people **who keep us safe**.

Read these sentences. Say if they are *true* or *false*.

a) A policeman helps to keep us safe. _____

b) A policeman keeps our homes safe. _____

c) A policeman wears a uniform on his head. _____

d) A policeman wears a cap on his feet. _____

e) A policeman helps children to keep safe on the road. _____

f) A policeman is friends with robbers. _____

g) A policeman sometimes drives a police car. _____

h) A policeman sets fire to houses. _____

i) A police station is where firemen meet. _____

Fighting a fire

Remember

Many **adverbs** end with '**ly**'. The words often describe **how** something happens.

The fire burnt **brightly**.

1 Do the word sums. Write the words you make.

a) bright   + ly = <u>brightly</u>

b) immediate + ly = _____

c) quick   + ly = _____

d) loud   + ly = _____

e) sudden   + ly = _____

f) brave   + ly = _____

g) safe   + ly = _____

h) slow   + ly = _____

2 Read the story. Write an 'ly' word in each gap.

The fire grew and grew. It shone <u>brightly</u> (bright) in the night sky. The whole house was on fire! As soon as she saw the fire, Anna _____ (immediate) telephoned the fire station. The fire truck came _____ (quick). The driver sounded the truck's siren _____ (loud) to warn people. _____ (Sudden) there was a shout from inside the building. Two people were trapped! The firemen _____ (brave) rescued two people and got them _____ (safe) out of the house. The firemen _____ (slow) got the fire under control.

I can see ...

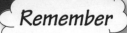

We use **is** and **are** in the **present tense**.

The baker ~~are~~ is baking bread.

1 **Choose the correct verb to complete each sentence.**

a) A shopkeeper _____ (is, are) standing outside his shop.

b) A truck driver _____ (is, are) loading boxes onto his truck.

c) There _____ (is, are) lots of vans in the street.

d) The butcher _____ (is, are) selling meat.

e) Some children _____ (is, are) running to school.

2 **Rewrite these sentences correctly.**

a) A lady are carrying a baby.

_____

b) Three people is drinking coffee.

_____

c) A man are walking through the park.

_____

d) The boats is in the harbour.

_____

e) A few men is fishing.

_____

Some things I saw yesterday

Remember

We use **was** and **were**
in the **past tense**.

The builders ~~was~~ were
building a new house.

1 **Choose the correct verb to complete each sentence.**

a) A boy _____ (was, were) talking to a girl.

b) Some birds _____ (was, were) in the yard.

c) A mechanic _____ (was, were) mending a car.

d) Lots of people _____ (was, were) on the bus.

e) A man _____ (was, were) selling newspapers.

2 **Rewrite these sentences correctly.**

a) A few ladies was doing some shopping.

_____

b) One man were looking in the shop window.

_____

c) A farmer were planting some seeds.

_____

d) Several goats was in the field.

_____

e) Some children was swimming in the sea.

_____

We can write a **verb** in the **present tense** in **two ways.**

A dog barks. A dog is barking.

1 **Write the verb in each sentence in the present tense in two ways.**

a) A car ___hoots___ (hoot).

A car _is hooting_ (hoot).

b) A child _____ (shout).

A child _____ (shout).

c) A telephone _____ (ring).

A telephone _____ (ring).

d) A plane _____ (zoom).

A plane _____ (zoom).

2 **Write the correct form of the verb.**

a) A motorbike _____ (roar).

Some motorbikes are _____ (roar).

b) A door _____ (bang).

Two doors are _____ (bang).

c) A clock _____ (tick).

All the clocks are _____ (tick).

d) A bird _____ (sing).

Many birds are _____ (sing).

Sounds in the countryside

Remember

Verbs in the **past tense** often end in '**ed**'.

A lion roar**ed**.

1 **Write the past tense of each verb.**

a) Some bees __buzzed__ (buzz) around some flowers.

b) A horse _____ (neigh).

c) Birds _____ (chirp) in the trees.

d) A frog _____ (croak).

e) The flock of birds _____ (flap) their wings.

f) The farmer _____ (push) his wheelbarrow.

2 **Rewrite the sentences. Change the verbs into the past tense.**

a) The mouse squeaks.

_____

b) Early in the morning a cockerel crows.

_____

c) Some cows moo.

_____

d) The children shout as they splash in the stream.

_____

e) A man chops down a tree.

_____

f) The men bang their drums.

_____

In the park

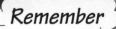

Some **verbs** in the **past tense** are **irregular** and do **not** end in '**ed**'.

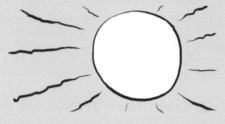

Yesterday the sun ~~**shined**~~ **shone** in the sky.

1 **Choose the correct form of the verb to complete each sentence.**

    a) I _____ (felt, feeled) very happy.

    b) I _____ (buyed, bought) some bread.

    c) I _____ (took, taked) it to the park.

    d) I _____ (sitted, sat) on a bench.

    e) I _____ (breaked, broke) the bread into pieces.

2 **Write these sentences correctly. The verb is spelled incorrectly in each.**

    a) I throwed the bread onto the grass.

    _____

    b) Some birds flied down from the trees.

    _____

    c) They eated some of the bread.

    _____

    d) I drinked some water from a fountain.

    _____

    e) Then I goed home.

    _____

We, our and us

When we talk about **ourselves**, we use the words **we**, **our** and **us.**

We are proud of **our** community. Come and visit **us**!

1 **Choose the correct word to complete the sentences.**

a) __We__ (We, Us) have a river in _____ (we, our) town.

b) Come for a swim with _____ (our, us) in the lake.

c) Do you like _____ (us, our) museum?

d) _____ (We, Us) think the library is very good.

e) _____ (Us, We) go to _____ (us, our) local school.

f) _____ (We, Our) teacher teaches _____ (us, we).

2 **Change the underlined words to make the sentences make sense. Use 'we', 'our' or 'us'.**

a) <u>Us</u> can catch fish in <u>we</u> pond. _____

b) Look at the statue in <u>us</u> town square. _____

c) Many tourists visit <u>we</u> in Jamaica. _____

d) Tourists love <u>us</u> beaches. _____

e) <u>Our</u> hope you have a good holiday. _____

f) <u>Us</u> took <u>we</u> umbrellas because it was raining. _____

Land forms

A **question** always **begins** with a **capital letter** and **ends** with a **question mark**.

1 Here are some questions about the place you live.

2 Choose the correct word to begin each sentence.

3 Fill in the missing question mark at the end of each sentence.

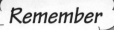

4 Write an answer for each question.

a) _____ (Is, Are) there any hills where you live__

_____

b) _____ (Is, Are) there a beach__

_____

c) _____ (Is, Are) there a stream__

_____

d) _____ (Is, Are) there any fields near your house__

_____

e) _____ (Is, Are) you near the sea__

_____

f) _____ (Is, Are) you near a wood or forest__

_____

g) _____ (Is, Are) there any ponds__

_____

h) _____ (Is, Are) any farms nearby__

Questions

1 **Read this poem.**

Remember

We all have lots of **BIG questions** about **ourselves** and our **world**!

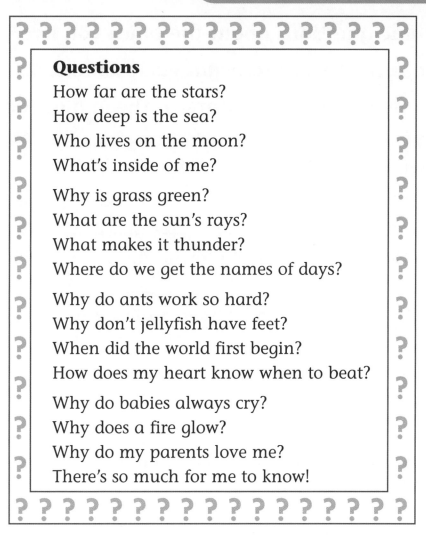

Questions

How far are the stars?
How deep is the sea?
Who lives on the moon?
What's inside of me?

Why is grass green?
What are the sun's rays?
What makes it thunder?
Where do we get the names of days?

Why do ants work so hard?
Why don't jellyfish have feet?
When did the world first begin?
How does my heart know when to beat?

Why do babies always cry?
Why does a fire glow?
Why do my parents love me?
There's so much for me to know!

2 **Think of two questions you would like answers to!**
Write them below.

_____

_____

_____

Questions with has/have, do/does

Remember

A **question** always **begins** with a **capital letter** and ends with a **question mark**.

1 Here are some questions about the place you live.

2 Choose the correct word to begin each sentence.

3 Fill in the missing question mark at the end of each sentence.

4 Write an answer for each question.

a) _Have_ (Has, Have) you got a library where you live__

_____

b) _____ (Do, Does) you have a town hall__

_____

c) _____ (Do, Does) your town have a museum__

_____

d) How many supermarkets _____ (has, have) your town got__

_____

e) _____ (Has, Have) your town got a cinema__

_____

f) _____ (Do, Does) you have a sports stadium__

_____

g) How many restaurants _____ (has, have) you got__

_____

People in the community

Remember

Naming words are called **nouns**.
A noun may be the name of
a **person**.

I am a sculptor.

1 **Match the names of these people and the jobs they do.**

1 sculptor

2 priest

3 carpenter

4 tailor

5 veterinarian

6 butcher

7 garbage collector

8 builder

9 mechanic

10 market trader

11 cashier

12 cook

a) I work in a church and teach people about God.

b) I make things from wood.

c) I make things like statues out of stone.

d) I sell meat.

e) I build houses.

f) I make clothes.

g) I look after sick animals.

h) I have a stall in a market.

i) I collect garbage and keep the streets clean.

j) I work in a bank.

k) I cook food.

l) I mend engines and work in a garage.

2 **Use a dictionary. Find out what opticians do. Write what they do.**

_____

_____

Places in the community

Remember

Naming words are called **nouns**.
A noun may be the name of a **place**.

A mechanic works in a **garage**.

1 **Write a sentence about each place.**

   a) museum — A museum is a place where we can see lots of interesting things.

   b) library _____

   c) supermarket _____

   d) factory _____

   e) church _____

   f) school _____

   g) garage _____

   h) town hall _____

   i) post office _____

   j) bank _____

2 **Here are the definitions of two places that begin with 'h'. Guess what they are.**

   a) _____ This is where sick people are cared for by doctors and nurses.

   b) _____ This is a place for ships and boats to stay.

Naming words are called **nouns**.
A noun may be the name of
a **thing**.

A **tank** is for storing water.

1 Sort these things into two sets.

> river   tank   ship   hill   bridge   tree
> tap   lake   road   rain   flag   sea

Man-made	Natural

2 Write the words in each set in alphabetical order.
natural things:

_____ _____ _____ _____ _____

man-made things:

_____ _____ _____ _____ _____

Remember

Rule 1: We often add 's' to the **end** of a **singular** noun to make it **plural**.   one bone – lots of bones

Rule 2: When a noun ends in 's', 'x', 'ch' or 'sh' we add 'es' to make it **plural**.   one dish – lots of dishes

Rule 3: In some words we change the 'y' to 'i' and add 'es' to make the **plural**.   one lady – lots of ladies

Complete this chart:

singular	plural
house	
baby	
beach	
study	
	bushes
	factories
mountain	
	farms
animal	
lorry	
arch	
	stories
box	
body	
glass	

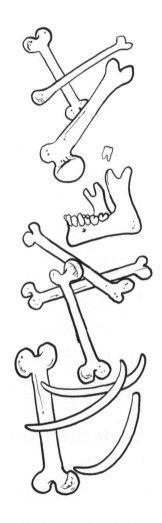

114

A bridge goes over a river

A **preposition** tells us the position of one thing in relation to another.

A bridge goes **over** a river.

1 Choose the correct preposition to complete each sentence.

a) The garage is _____ (between, over) a shop and an office.

b) A train goes _____ (between, through) a tunnel.

c) A bridge goes _____ (under, over) a river.

d) A doctor works _____ (in, on) a hospital.

e) Our yard is _____ (in, behind) our house.

f) A boat floats _____ (under, on) the water.

g) There is a lot of water _____ (above, in) the tank.

h) There is a lot of water _____ (behind, between) the dam.

i) A fish swims _____ (against, under) the water.

j) The plane flies _____ (under, above) the forest.

2 Underline the preposition 'hiding' in each set of letters.

a) abetweencd **b)** efthroughi **c)** jklmnxoncv

d) mnbvovertw **e)** dunderftgv **f)** zabehindqw

In town

Sometimes **poems** make us **think**.

1 Read this poem.

In town

People walking fast,
People walking slow,
People walking and talking,
Everywhere they go.

People talking quietly,
People shouting loud,
People in the market,
People in a crowd.

People driving cars,
People riding bikes,
People doing shopping
Buying anything they like.

Busy, busy, busy,
The town's too busy for me,
I think I prefer the countryside,
Or the quietness of the sea!

2 Think about this question:

Where would you prefer to live?

- in a busy town
- in the countryside
- by the sea

A range of mountains

Remember

Sometimes we have names for
a **number of things that
come together**.
a **range** of mountains

1 **Complete each sentence with the correct word.**

a) I bought a _____ (bunch, herd) of bananas.

b) In the sky I saw a _____ (fleet, flock) of birds.

c) The fishermen tried to catch the _____ (shoal, forest) of fish.

d) Near the village there was a _____ (library, forest) of trees.

e) Our school has a _____ (crowd, library) of books.

f) In the harbour there was a _____ (fleet, pack) of ships.

g) We played a game with a _____ (pile, pack) of cards.

h) You must walk up a _____ (flight, swarm) of steps.

i) On the beach there was a _____ (pile, pack) of stones.

j) A _____ (crowd, school) of people gathered in the town square.

2 **Underline the correct phrases.**

a) a flock of dolphins   a school of dolphins

b) a herd of goats   a shoal of goats

c) a swarm of flowers   a bunch of flowers

d) a pack of rocks   a pile of rocks

e) a staff of teachers   a class of teachers

f) a chest of bushes   a hedge of bushes

117

Caring for our community

Read this letter that Carla wrote to the local newspaper.

Remember

We are all **responsible** for **caring for our environment**.

15 King Street
Port Arthur
Jamaica

Dear Editor

I love our town but there is one thing I dislike very much. There is litter and rubbish everywhere in the town centre. It makes the town look dirty.

Our town gets lots of visitors. They come to see all our historic buildings. They spend a lot of money in our town. They stay in our hotels and buy things in our shops.

Also, rubbish is bad for the visitors and people who live in the town. There are swarms of flies when there is rubbish and litter everywhere. If it is not cleared up it will make people ill.

Litter is a danger to motorists, too. It can cause accidents. Broken glass can cut car tyres. Yesterday I fell over and cut myself on some broken glass in the town centre.

Yours sincerely

Carla Brown

Reading with understanding

Remember

It is important to **understand** what you read and to **think** about it.

Answer these questions about Carla's letter.

a) Where does Carla live?

_____

b) Who did she write to?

_____

c) Why do you think she wrote to the editor?

_____

d) What does Carla dislike very much about her town?

_____

e) Why does the town get lots of visitors?

_____

f) Where do they spend lots of money?

_____

g) Why is rubbish bad for visitors and people who live in town?

_____

h) Why is litter dangerous?

_____

Caring for our environment

Remember

We are all **responsible** for
caring for our environment.

1 Write some ways we can care for our environment
at home.

2 Write some ways we can care for our environment
at school.

How green are you?

1 Read these simple rules.

2 Decorate the border.

3 Copy the poster and stick up the rules at home for everyone to see!

Remember

We can **all** make the world a **better place** with a little effort!

- Don't leave the tap running when you brush your teeth.
- Turn off the TV at the set. Don't use a remote control.
- Make a shopping list. Don't just go and buy whatever you happen to see.
- Don't buy things with a lot of packaging.
- Have a shower instead of a bath.
- Switch off lights that are not needed.
- Try not to buy things that are disposable.
- Try to recycle as much glass and cardboard as possible.
- Walk more! (71% of all trips by car are under 5 kilometres!)
- Eat less meat.
- Use natural ventilation rather than air conditioning where possible.
- Eat more organic vegetables (which do not use chemicals when grown).

A modern building is new

Remember

An **adjective** is a describing word e.g. Kingston is a
big city. **Opposites** are words whose meanings are as
different as possible from each other e.g. *happy, sad.*

1 **Choose the best adjective to complete each sentence.**

  a) The modern building was _____ (new, old).

  b) The building was not a long way away. It was
     _____ (far, near).

  c) A brick is _____ (hard, soft).

  d) A broad river is _____ (wide, narrow).

  e) A mountain is _____ (tiny, huge).

  f) An attractive view is _____ (pretty, ugly).

  g) There was a storm. The sea was _____
     (rough, smooth).

  h) A loud sound is _____ (quiet, noisy).

  i) I could not stop reading the book. It was _____
     (interesting, boring).

  j) A glass that contains nothing is _____ (full, empty).

  k) When it is night it is _____ (light, dark).

  l) The dog ate too much and was _____ (fat, thin).

2 **Write the opposite of each adjective.**

  a) noisy _____   **b)** near _____   **c)** old _____

  d) rough _____   **e)** ugly _____   **f)** soft _____

  g) huge _____   **h)** wide _____   **i)** boring _____

  j) fat _____   **k)** dark _____   **l)** empty _____

Remember

1 **Read some interesting facts about Jamaica.**

An **adjective** is a describing word.

Kingston is a **big** city.

- Kingston is the biggest city in Jamaica.
- Mandeville is smaller than Kingston.
- Blue Mountain Peak is the highest point in Jamaica.
- Catherine's Peak is lower than Blue Mountain Peak.
- Rio Minho is the longest river in Jamaica.
- Hope River is shorter than Rio Minho.
- Kingston Harbour is the largest harbour in Jamaica.
- Port Antonio Harbour is smaller than Kingston Harbour.

2 **Answer these questions.**

a) Is Kingston smaller than Mandeville?

_____

b) Is Blue Mountain Peak lower than Catherine's Peak?

_____

c) Is Rio Minho shorter than Hope River?

_____

d) Is Kingston Harbour smaller than Port Antonio Harbour?

_____

3 **Read about some old buildings in Jamaica.**

Devon House in Kingston was built in 1889.
Fort Charles in Port Royal was built in 1662.
St James Cathedral in Spanish Town was built in 1523.

Plant words

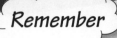
Remember

> There are **five vowels.**
> They are:
>
> **a e i o u**
>
> Every word must contain **at least one** vowel.
> Sometimes the letter **y** acts as a **part-time vowel**
> (e.g. family).

Read the meaning of each word.
Then fill in the missing vowels in the words.

a) t _ m b _ r   wood

b) l _ _ f   a flat, green part of a plant or tree

c) t r _ n k   a main part of a tree

d) b r _ n c h   the part of a tree that sticks out from the trunk

e) r _ _ t   the part of a plant that is under the ground

f) s t _ m   the main part of a plant above ground

g) s _ _ d   plants grow from these

h) c _ c _ n _ t   grows on a palm tree

i) c _ c t _ s   a thick plant covered with prickles

j) h _ r b   a plant used in cooking to give flavour

Sorting the words out

These words are in **alphabetical order,** according to their **first** letters:

brother **f**ather **m**other

These words all **begin** with the **same** letter.

They are in **alphabetical order**, according to their **second** letters:

b**a**th b**e**d b**r**other

---

1 **Write these words in alphabetical order, according to their first letters.**

a) logwood cedar   rosewood mahoe

_____ _____ _____ _____

b) ebony   palm   breadfruit mango

_____ _____ _____ _____

c) soursop banana grapes   papaya

_____ _____ _____ _____

2 **Write these words in alphabetical order, according to their second letters.**

a) pear   pomegranate plum

_____ _____ _____

b) cabbage coconut cherry

_____ _____ _____

c) crocus   coffee   cactus

_____ _____ _____

It's a mango tree

We sometimes **join two words together** and **miss out some letters**.

It's (It is) a mango tree.

1 Match the words.   Write them here.

a) I'm   he is   _____

b) you're   we are   _____

c) he's   I am   I'm _____ I am

d) she's   it is   _____

e) it's   you are   _____

f) we're   they are   _____

g) they're   she is   _____

2 Complete each sentence correctly.

a) The girl is crying because _____ (he's, she's) unhappy.

b) Apples are lovely. _____ (We're, They're) always sweet.

c) _____ (You're, It's) a tall tree.

d) My friend called for me. _____ (We're, You're) going to school.

e) I am in the garden. _____ (I'm, It's) planting some seeds.

Old Noah and his Ark

Remember

Poems and **rhymes** can be a **lot of fun!**

1 Read and enjoy this rhyme.

Old Noah built a wooden ark,
To put the animals in.
Some were quiet, some were noisy,
And some made quite a din.

The animals went in one by one,
The elephant was eating a currant bun.

The animals went in two by two,
The crocodile and the kangaroo.

The animals went in three by three,
The tall giraffe and the tiny flea.

The animals went in four by four,
The fat hippopotamus stuck in the door.

The animals went in five by five,
The bear and some bees in their hive.

The animals went in six by six,
The monkey played lots of tricks.

The animals went in seven by seven,
The ant said to the elephant, 'Who are
  you shoving?'

The animals went in eight by eight,
Some were early, some were late.

The animals went in nine by nine,
The hedgehog and the porcupine.

The animals went in ten by ten,
If you want any more, you can read it again!

Animal noises

Remember

1 Write each sentence correctly.
Underline the verb in each sentence.

> Many **verbs** are **doing words**.
> Cats **miaow**.

a) Goats roar. | Goats <u>bray</u>.

b) Cows quack. | _____

c) Lions bray. | _____

d) Dogs croak. | _____

e) Ducks bark. | _____

f) Frogs chatter. | _____

g) Parrots moo. | _____

h) Elephants squawk. | _____

i) Monkeys squeak. | _____

j) Mice trumpet. | _____

2 Write each verb in the past tense.

a) The goats __brayed__ (bray).

b) The cows _____ (moo).

c) The lions _____ (roar).

d) The dogs _____ (bark).

e) The ducks _____ (quack).

f) The frogs _____ (croak).

g) The parrots _____ (squawk).

h) The elephants _____ (trumpet).

i) The monkeys _____ (chatter).

j) The mice _____ (squeak).

Animals and their young

The names of some animals and their young are **different**. A **cat** has **kittens**.

1 Match the animal with its baby.

a) dog	kitten
b) cat	lamb
c) hen	puppy
d) sheep	kid
e) goat	chick
f) cow	foal
g) horse	tadpole
h) duck	calf
i) frog	cub
j) lion	duckling

Write the animal and its baby here.

_____ and _____

_____ and _____

dog and _puppy_

_____ and _____

_____ and _____

_____ and _____

_____ and _____

_____ and _____

_____ and _____

_____ and _____

2 Complete each sentence with the correct word.

a) A young duck is called a _____.

b) A young horse is called a _____.

c) A young goat is called a _____.

d) A young cat is called a _____.

e) A young hen is called a _____.

f) A young frog is called a _____.

g) A young lion is called a _____.

h) A young cow is called a _____.

i) A young dog is called a _____.

j) A young is sheep called a _____.

The baby chick

It is important to **understand what we read**.

Number these sentences to tell how a baby chick is born.

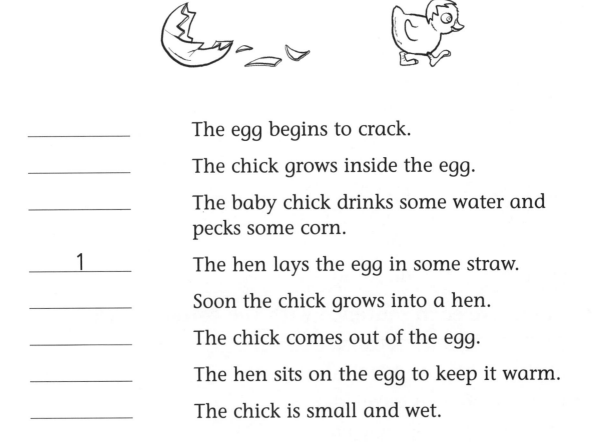

_____ The egg begins to crack.

_____ The chick grows inside the egg.

_____ The baby chick drinks some water and pecks some corn.

____1____ The hen lays the egg in some straw.

_____ Soon the chick grows into a hen.

_____ The chick comes out of the egg.

_____ The hen sits on the egg to keep it warm.

_____ The chick is small and wet.

Pets, farm animals and wild animals

Remember

It is important to be able to **sort** things into **sets**.

1   Write these animals in the correct place on the chart.

chicken	crocodile	parrot	monkey	elephant
sheep	giraffe	horse	cat	lion
cow	dog	goat		

pets	farm animals	wild animals

2   Add the names of some more animals to each set.

Animal alphabet

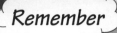
Remember

Lots of books, like **encyclopedias**, are **arranged in alphabetical order**.

1 The meanings below are muddled up.
Write the correct meaning next to each animal.

Aa	alligator	This animal can hop and croak. This animal lives in rivers. It has sharp teeth.
Bb	bear	This animal looks like a small horse.
Cc	camel	This animal has two tusks and a trunk.
Dd	donkey	This large wild animal has thick fur.
Ee	elephant	This animal lives in the desert.
Ff	frog	This animal lives in rivers. It has sharp teeth.

2 Continue the list with some animals of your own.
Write a sentence about each of your animals.

Gg _____ _____

Hh _____ _____

Ii _____ _____

Jj _____ _____

Kk _____ _____

Animal riddles

Remember

When we read we must always **look for clues** to help us understand.

1 Read the riddles. Write the name of each animal.

> giraffe   cat   panda   elephant   sheep   crocodile

a)
I am soft and furry.
I have sharp claws.
I wag my tail when I am angry.
I purr when I am happy.
What am I?
I am a _____

b)
I have four long legs.
I have a long neck.
I have small ears.
I eat leaves from the top of trees.
What am I?
I am a _____

c)
I live in rivers.
I am strong.
I have a tough green skin.
I have short legs and sharp teeth.
What am I?
I am a _____

d)
I live in the jungle.
I may be brown or grey.
I am a very big animal.
I have big ears and a long trunk.
What am I?
I am an _____

e)
I have a white curly coat.
My coat is made of wool.
I like to eat grass.
My young are called lambs.
What am I?
I am a _____

f)
I am black and white.
I am found in China.
I am a shy animal.
I eat bamboo.
What am I?
I am a _____

Growing some flowers

We add '**ed**' to some verbs to make them into the **past tense** e.g. plant – planted.
Some verbs have **irregular** past tenses e.g. give – gave.

1 **Write the past tense of each verb in each sentence.**

a) I _bought_ (buy) some seeds in a packet.

b) I _____ (go) into the garden.

c) I _____ (dig) a hole in the soil with a spade.

d) I _____ (open) the packet.

e) I _____ (plant) the seeds.

f) I _____ (fill) the hole with some soil.

g) I _____ (give) them some water every day.

h) The sun _____ (shine) every day.

i) Soon I _____ (see) some little green shoots.

j) Each day the flowers _____ (grow) bigger and bigger.

k) One day I _____ (pick) some flowers.

l) I _____ (give) them to my mum.

m) My mum _____ (be) very pleased.

n) She _____ (put) the flowers in a vase.

o) The flowers _____ (look) very nice.

2 **Read the sentences again. They make a story!**

Trees

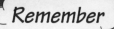

Reading for information is important.

1 **Read this information about trees.**

What is a tree?

A tree is a plant. Some trees grow very tall. Some trees are very old.

What are the parts of a tree?

The main part of a tree is the trunk.

Branches grow from the trunk.

Smaller branches are called twigs.

Leaves grow from the twigs.

The roots of the tree are under the ground.

The roots give the tree water.

How do trees help us?

Lots of animals and insects make their homes in trees.

We make things from the wood from trees.

We eat the fruit from trees.

2 **Choose the correct word for each gap.**

   a) A tree is a _____. (reptile, plant)

   b) The main part of the tree is the _____. (root, trunk)

   c) _____ (Branches, Twigs) grow from the trunk.

   d) Smaller branches are called _____. (trunks, twigs)

   e) _____ (Leaves, Roots) grow from the twigs.

   f) The _____ (branches, roots) of the tree are under the ground.

   g) The roots give the tree _____. (water, wood)

   h) Lots of _____ (people, insects) make their homes in trees.

135

Remember

Correct **punctuation** in **sentences** is important.

1 **Write some sentences of your own.**

a) Why are trees important?

_____

_____

b) How many different trees can you name?

_____

_____

c) Name some things we make from wood.

_____

_____

d) Name some fruit that grows on trees.

_____

_____

e) Name some animals that live in or near trees.

_____

_____

2 **Write the missing commas in these lists.**

a) trunks branches twigs and roots

b) pink red blue and yellow

c) cat dog mouse and rabbit

d) apple banana pear and orange

e) plate cup saucer and bowl

f) book comic magazine and letter

Bananas

1 Choose the correct word to complete each sentence.

Sentences must **make sense**.

a) Bananas are very good for _____ (us, it).

b) _____ (You, They) are full of vitamins and minerals.

c) _____ (His, Our) bodies need vitamins and minerals.

d) A banana tree is not a tree at all. _____ (She, It) is really a large plant.

e) The 'trunk' is not made of wood. _____ (It, He) is made of leaves.

2 Write what each underlined word stands for.

a) Bananas are still green when <u>they</u> <u>(the bananas)</u> are cut.

b) Bananas are packed into boxes. The boxes are put onto a truck and <u>they</u> (_____) are taken to the port.

c) A crane picks up the boxes of bananas. <u>It</u> (_____) loads them onto a banana boat.

d) The boxes of bananas are put into cool rooms on the boat. <u>They</u> (_____) stop the bananas from getting ripe.

e) The captain of the boat is an important man. <u>He</u> (_____) makes sure the boat sails safely.

Thanksgiving

Remember

It is important to be **thankful** for **animals** and **plants**.

1 **Read this thank-you for the cow.**

Thank you for the gentle cow,
that eats grass all day.

Thank you for its big brown eyes,
that look at me softly.

Thank you for the milk it gives us,
that can be made into cream, cheese,
butter and yogurt.

Thank you for the meat it provides
that can be made into delicious meals.

Thank you for its skin,
that can be made into leather for shoes.

2 **Write your own thank-you for another animal or for a plant or tree.**

_____

_____

_____

_____

_____

_____

Syllables

Remember

When we say a word slowly we can break it down into **smaller parts** called **syllables**.

bam/boo   bamboo

1 **These words have been broken into two syllables. Write each word correctly.**

a) gar/den   _garden_   **b)** flow/er   _____

c) man/go   _____   **d)** rose/wood   _____

e) sour/sop   _____   **f)** bread/fruit   _____

g) wil/low   _____   **h)** ack/ee   _____

i) mar/ket   _____   **j)** dol/phin   _____

k) thir/sty   _____   **l)** sis/ter   _____

m) win/dow   _____   **n)** pen/cil   _____

2 **The syllables in these words are back to front. Write each word correctly.**

a) dow/win   _window_   **b)** ter/sis   _____

c) cil/pen   _____   **d)** den/gar   _____

e) go/man   _____   **f)** sop/sour   _____

g) low/wil   _____   **h)** ket/mar   _____

i) sty/thir   _____   **j)** er/flow   _____

k) wood/rose   _____   **l)** fruit/bread   _____

m) ee/ack   _____   **n)** phin/dol   _____

Test 3

1 Underline the correct answer:

a reporter: **a)** bakes bread **b)** reports the news ☐

2 Choose the best adverb to complete the sentence. ☐

The man shouted _____ (angrily, quietly) at the motorist.

3 Write this sentence correctly: ☐

Some goats is climbing over some rocks.

_____

4 Choose the correct verb to complete this sentence: ☐

There _____ (was, were) twenty birds in the tree.

5 Write the past tense of the verb: ☐

Yesterday I _____ (hop) to the shop.

6 Write the past tense of the verb: ☐

Last week I _____ (dig) a big hole.

7 Complete this sentence correctly. ☐

Pam and Anna said, '_____ (We, Us) like _____ (our, us) picture the best.'

8 Complete this question with either 'Is' or 'Are'. ☐

_____ there thirty days in September?

9 Complete this question with either 'Do' or 'Does'. ☐

_____ an elephant have a trunk?

10 Say if the underlined noun is the name of a place or a thing. ☐

The harbour was full of boats. _____

11 Write the plural of these nouns:

    a) arch _____   **b)** lady _____

12 Choose the best preposition to complete the sentence.

    The children hid _____ (through, behind) the tree.

13 Complete this phrase correctly:

    a _____ (bunch, pile) of bananas

14 What adjective means the opposite of 'low'? _____

15 Write the correct form of the adjective:

    Cuba is _____ (big) than Jamaica.

16 Underline the word that means 'was not'

    isn't   weren't   wasn't

17 Change the underlined verb to the past tense.

    The parrots <u>squawk</u> _____ in the jungle all day.

18 Underline the young of a sheep:

    kid   foal   lamb   calf

19 Fill in the missing commas:

    On the farm I saw some cows sheep goats horses and pigs.

20 Fill in the missing syllable to make the name of a fruit: lem__

Scoring:
Each question is worth 1 mark.   Complete this:
Mark your test.   **I scored ____ out of 20.**

High Frequency Word List

How many of these high frequency words can you read?

about	been	dig	half	jump
after	big	do	has	just
again	boy	don't	have	last
all	brother	dog	he	laugh
an	but	door	help	like
and	by	down	her	little
another	call	first	here	live
are	came	for	him	look
as	can	from	his	love
at	can't	get	home	made
away	cat	girl	house	make
back	could	good	how	man
ball	come	go	if	many
be	dad	going	in	may
because	day	got	is	me
bed	did	had	it	more

High Frequency Word List

much	or	she	three	were
mum	our	should	time	what
must	out	sister	to	when
my	over	so	too	where
name	people	some	took	who
new	play	take	tree	will
next	pull	than	two	with
night	push	that	up	would
no	put	the	us	yes
not	ran	their	very	you
now	run	them	want	your
of	said	then	was	
off	saw	there	water	
old	school	these	way	
on	see	they	we	
once	seen	this	went	

Thematic Word Lists

Days of the week
Monday Tuesday Wednesday Thursday Friday Saturday Sunday

Months of the year
January	February	March	April	May	June
July	August	September	October	November	December

Seasons
spring summer autumn winter

Family
father		mother	brother sister	baby	grandmother
grandfather	aunt	uncle	cousin	nephew	niece

Jobs
astronaut	author	baker	builder	butcher	cook
dentist	doctor	farmer	fire-fighter	mechanic	nurse
pilot	plumber	policeman	postman	teacher	vet

Animals
bear	bird	butterfly	camel	cat	cow	crocodile
dog	donkey	duck	elephant	fish	fox	frog
giraffe	goat	hen	horse	kangaroo	lion	monkey
mouse	panda	pig	rabbit	rat	sheep	snake
tiger	turtle	whale	wolf			

Action words
bite	break	build	catch	climb	cook
cry	cut	dance	dig	draw	drink
eat	fall	give	help	hide	hit
hop	jump	kick	kiss	laugh	mend
play	pull	read	ride	run	see
shut	sing	sit	sleep	swim	talk
think	throw	walk	wash	whisper	write